CONFESSIONS

Tales of Female Misbehaviour

mischief

This novel is entirely a work of fiction.
The names, characters and incidents portrayed in it are
the work of the author's imagination. Any resemblance to
actual persons, living or dead, events or localities is
entirely coincidental.

Mischief
An imprint of HarperCollins*Publishers*
77–85 Fulham Palace Road,
Hammersmith, London W6 8JB

www.mischiefbooks.com

A Paperback Original 2013

First published in Great Britain in ebook format by
HarperCollins*Publishers* 2012

Copyright
Neighborhood Watch © Lolita Lopez
The Shop © Lisette Ashton
Come In Handy © Heather Towne
Hard Copy © Elizabeth Coldwell
Interview With The Vamp © Scarlett Rush
The Going Down Chronicles © Chrissie Bentley
A Big So Long to Innocence © Kim Mitchell
Mr Flint © Primula Bond
The Method © Justine Elyot
Keeping a Promise © Jenny Swallows

The author asserts the moral right to
be identified as the author of this work

A catalogue record for this book is
available from the British Library

ISBN-13: 9780007553129

CONTENTS

Contents

Neighborhood Watch
Lolita Lopez

The chirping alarm clock on my cell phone interrupted my study time. A frisson of excitement rippled through my belly as I realized it was time. I set aside my textbook and notes and stretched my aching neck. Becoming a petroleum engineer had always been a dream of mine, especially since I'd grown up in the oil and gas booms and busts of West Texas, but the graduate classes had proven grueling and less than exciting at times.

Sometimes I needed to blow off a little steam. Some people went running or had a massage or even teamed up for a no-holds-barred game of paintball. Me? I preferred something a bit more wild and risky. All my life I'd enjoyed the attention of others. Pageants, plays, cheerleading – I'd always found ways to feed that need for all eyes to be on me.

Here in college, I'd discovered new possibilities for

1

my exhibitionist predilections. My poor, Sunday-school-teachin' mama would have died from a heart attack if she'd discovered what her sweet little baby girl got up to every third Friday of the month, but I just couldn't stop myself. It was too exhilarating.

So I pushed up off the couch in my apartment's small living room and headed toward my bedroom. The skimpy outfit I'd chosen greeted me. I rubbed the whisper-soft silk against my cheek. This was one of my simpler pieces, just a halter-top babydoll made of pleated georgette and silk with a matching thong.

I stripped out of my yoga pants and camisole and slipped into the flimsy lingerie. I loved the way the fabric clung to my curves. It made me feel sexy in a classy sort of way. The tiny thong fit snugly between my ass cheeks and cupped my already throbbing clit. Anticipation made my belly wobble uncontrollably. My pussy pulsed with need. Slick wetness seeped from my core. I couldn't wait to get out on that balcony and masturbate for my small throng of enthusiastic fans.

My fingers found the black elastic band holding my dark hair in a high ponytail. I gave my head a shake and combed my fingers through the waves. Before I left my bedroom, I put on the matching kimono and grabbed the folded towel containing the selection of toys from the end of the bed. I switched off the light in my room and returned to the living area.

From practice runs and comments from my fans, I knew which lights in the living room to leave on and which to snuff out before I made my way to the balcony. Too much light, and I drew unwanted attention. Not enough light, and the show was too dark for the guys and gals in the opposite apartment building to enjoy.

Out on the balcony, I shut the glass door behind me and stood still for a moment, allowing my eyes to adjust to the darkness. I cast one quick glance to the balconies opposite mine and noticed the lounging fans. Some were couples, but most were groups of single guys and girls who rented the three- and four-bedroom apartments over there. Our buildings were the last two in the complex and situated just perfectly for my naughty stripteases. We were surrounded by trees and a woodsy area and sheltered from the louder and usually bustling pool, gym and recreational center.

Though I pretended not to notice my viewers, I trembled just as wildly as the first night I'd done this. Back then, it had been an impromptu decision borne out of pure boredom and desperation. A dry spell between boyfriends and the stress of finals had killed my usually raging libido. I'd tried and tried to get my juices flowing again with vibrators and videos and erotica, but nothing had worked.

Then, that fateful night in May, I'd been outside enjoying a beer and the quiet stillness of the night when

I'd heard my downstairs neighbors going at it like a pair of horny weasels. There was something so illicitly dirty about listening in to their session of bed-breaking sex. In minutes, I'd been soaking through my panties. My fingers had quickly found the right rhythm and, in no time at all, I was coming so hard.

When I'd finished, I heard the first whistles and applause from the balcony opposite mine. I'd been mortified and felt sure I would die of embarrassment. But then, ever so slowly, I'd experienced the strangest surge of accomplishment and pride. I'd given the guys across the way a nice bow and wave before darting into the house where I'd fallen on to my couch and laughed myself hoarse. Suddenly, I couldn't wait to do it again.

Once a month seemed like the perfect balance to the issue of supply and demand for my balcony peep shows. Anything more and I risked the crowds getting too big and someone sending a nasty note to the complex's office. Or calling the cops. I enjoyed the limelight, of course, but spending a night in the slammer because I'd been caught rubbing my pussy in public wouldn't look so great on those résumés I was going to have to send out at some point in the near future.

A flashlight beam clicked on and off twice. I smiled at the silly signal the two original fans from Building F had come up with the second night I'd come out on to the balcony. I picked up the flashlight I kept on the

4

mosaic-topped bistro table and flashed them three times. My fingers pressed play on the iPod stereo system I'd stashed outside earlier. The hiphop playlist I'd chosen spilled out of the speakers. I didn't want noise complaints, but I needed the thudding pulse of the music to lend just the right vibe to my performance.

I placed the towel on the table with the flashlight and unwrapped the toys hidden inside the plush cotton. My heart leapt at the sight of the nipple clamps, lube and the double-penetrating dildo I'd picked up at the sex shop. It was one of those intimidating rubber toys that I was sure had been modeled after a pair of hung-like-a-horse porn stars.

Playing with it the first time had left me sweating and clutching at my sheets. There was nothing like the overwhelming sensation of being taken in both holes, my body stretched and filled to breaking point. Someday, I promised myself, I was going to play that game in the flesh. For now, the rubber fantasy version would have to do.

Keenly aware of my audience, I shed the kimono ever so slowly and revealed the gorgeous lingerie I'd chosen especially for them. I imagined their eyes lighting up at the sight of the purple georgette against my tan skin. My fingers hooked the silver chain of the nipple clamps and lifted them from the towel.

As if simply enjoying the cool night air, I walked over

to the balcony railing and leaned against it. I inhaled deeply, pulling the scent of honeysuckle and cedar into my lungs. My hands skimmed my curves through the thin material, the silver chain jangling as the nipple clamps dangling from my fingers rode the outline of my breasts and belly. I let my other hand slide between my thighs. Already the lacy fabric hugging my pussy was damp with the nectar dripping from my cunt. I teasingly rubbed my clit through the thong. I loved the way the material enhanced the stimulation, lending a sharper sensation to my circling fingers.

Wanting to stay on the edge, I slowly abandoned my pussy and allowed my hands to move up toward my breasts. I cupped the heavy flesh and thumbed my nipples through the silky cloth. My hands dipped behind the fabric and bared my breasts. The cool air and my arousal made the dusky-pink skin tighten to hard pebbles. I sucked my fingers until they were wet before using the slick pads to tweak my nipples.

Trial and error had led to my discovery that I enjoyed the kinkier side of breast play. My sensitive tits responded so well to the sensual torture of clamps, and I just couldn't get enough of them. I twisted the barrels on the underside of the silver clamps to open the teeth just enough to slide my hard nipples between them. I adjusted the pressure on the clamps until they were just right.

My pussy flooded at the sharp sensation of the clamps

squeezing the stiff peaks. The pain took my breath away, made my bare toes curl against the rough stone of the balcony floor. I inhaled shuddery breaths as I grew accustomed to the bite of the clamps. The squeezing sensation traveled from my nipples straight to my swollen clit.

I gave a little tug on the chain and gasped. The pleasure of such piercing discomfort sent my arousal into overdrive. Suddenly, I wasn't alone on the balcony. The fantasy of being tormented by two lovers swamped the reality of my peep show. My hands were their hands. My twisted, dirty thoughts were theirs.

With the finesse of a dancer, I turned and presented my back to the audience. I took a few steps toward the armless chair near the bistro table. My fingers slid under the skirt of the babydoll and grasped the sides of the thong. Bending over, I made sure to take my time as I peeled the thong down my backside and let it drop to my ankles. My hands glided over the bare cheeks of my ass. I gave each cheek a playful swat before standing tall and kicking aside the thong dangling from my ankles.

I sat on the chair and let my thighs fall apart. The cool night air kissed my blazing hot skin. I cupped my waxed mound and petted the smooth skin. My fingers slipped between the silky, wet lips of my sex. I explored every inch of my pussy. Slippery cream swirled beneath my fingertips. I lifted my hand to my mouth and tasted the salty essence of my cunt.

Moaning, I licked my fingers clean before putting them back on my sex. This time I penetrated my pussy, first with two fingers and then three. I flicked my clit, ramping up my lust as my digits plunged in and out of my tight passage. My fingers slid lower to my anus and circled the rosebud. My breath hitched at the forbidden sensation my fingers evoked.

A quiver of excitement pierced my lower belly. Anal play was one of my newer adventures. It still felt so deliciously dirty to experiment with toys and fingers and cocks up my backside. I figured my rather religious and conservative upbringing contributed to the feelings of extreme naughtiness that accompanied the act. Not that I much cared about the whys of my fascination with anal stimulation. It just felt so fucking good.

I reached for the small tube of lubricant on the towel and squirted a big dollop on my fingers. While I strummed my clit, I prepared myself for the intrusion of the dildos. My fingers worked the snug ring of muscle until it was ready to accept something quite a bit larger.

My heart beat so fast I couldn't hear anything over the rush of blood pounding against my eardrums. Pussy pulsing, I wrapped my slick fingers around the double dildo. The sex toy felt so heavy in my small hand. Holding it by the suction-cup base, I dragged the thick heads of the fake cocks through my wet pussy. My mouth gaped at the wicked sensation of the dildos sliding up and down and side to side through my cunt. It was too much, and, yet, not enough.

Gulping, I stood up and attached the dildo's base to the seat of my chair. I tested the suction before lowering myself on to the pair of fat rubber cocks. I pressed the tip of the longer one against the entrance to my pussy. The slick juice coating my skin eased its penetration. Fitting the other cock into place took some maneuvering. Finally, it popped inside my tight asshole. 'Oh!'

Biting my lower lip, I swallowed inch after glorious inch of those cocks. My pussy and ass stretched to accommodate the length and girth of both dildos. I loved the burn and swiveled my hips as I sank down to the base of the toy. For a few moments, I simply sat still and enjoyed the fullness. I closed my eyes and pretended I was seated on one lover's lap while the other knelt between my thighs and plunged his cock in and out of my pussy.

Tugging the nipple chain, I bounced slowly at first, while strumming my clit. It wasn't going to take much to send me over the edge. I rocked back and forth on the cocks. The chair squeaks mixed with the pumping bass of the music filtering out of the speakers. I flicked my stiff nub faster and faster until the panicky, shuddery feeling invaded my belly.

Seconds later, I groaned noisily as I came hard. My pussy juice gushed around the rubber dildo slamming in and out of me. My ass clamped rhythmically around the shaft buried there. It was wild and wicked and so fucking wonderful.

And I didn't want it to end. I refused to settle for just one orgasm. I wanted more, demanded more, from my pussy. My aching breasts begged for attention so I jerked on the chain connected to the clamps biting my nipples. The hard, sharp pain sent me rushing into the waves of another climax. I slapped a hand over my mouth as I howled my release, pussy fluttering and belly clenching as I came and came and came.

Awash in ecstasy, I rode those two rubber cocks until my thighs burned from exertion. I collapsed back against the shockingly cold metal of the chair and tried to catch my breath. Hand over my face, I sank down from the heights of pleasure and became aware of the raucous applause and whistling from the balconies opposite me. Grinning at a job well done, I gave myself a mental pat on the back.

Wincing, I gently pulled away from the double penetration of the dildos. I experienced an instant sensation of emptiness. It was crazy, but I already wanted those cocks inside me again. The sheen of sweat on my skin quickly cooled my body temperature and forced me to reach for the kimono. Brain still saturated with oxytocin, I smiled as I gathered up my props and turned off the music. I gave my adoring crowd a bow before slipping back inside my apartment and closing the blinds.

I dropped into the nearest plush chair and tossed the sex toys and towel on to the couch. Cringing, I unscrewed the clamps and hissed as blood rushed into the starved vessels. The clamps found their way to the floor. I pressed my palms to my poor, abused nipples and waited for the discomfort to pass.

The insides of my thighs were coated with my honey. I was thinking about taking a nice, hot, relaxing bath when my doorbell rang. Annoyed by the thought of unwanted night visitors, I considered ignoring it and ducking into my bathroom. The idea that it might be something important pulled me from my comfy chair and across the living room.

I rose on tiptoes to peer through the peephole and stepped back with surprise. Jay and Craig, the two guys who lived in the apartment building directly across from me, stood on my doorstep. We weren't strangers, but we were hardly friendly. I ran into them every now and then in the parking lot or laundry room, but we never did more than exchange amused glances before heading our separate ways. Why in the world were the two of them standing on my welcome mat now?

I wrapped the kimono tightly around my body, a ridiculous act considering they'd already seen everything I had to offer, and unlocked the door. The pair loomed in my doorway, their broad chests taking up all of the space. There was no mistaking the hunger in their gazes as they raked my body with a lingering stare. Suddenly embarrassed, I smiled uneasily. 'Uh, hey?'

'Hey,' they answered in near unison.

Jay spoke first. 'We're your neighbors.'

'I know.'

Jay's cheeks looked darker as he smiled sheepishly. 'Yeah, I guess you do.' He rubbed the back of his head and seemed uncomfortable. 'I'm just going to come right out and say it. Seems kind of silly to beat around the bush, right? We think you're amazing, and what you do out there is just – wow. I mean, *wow*.'

My expression softened at his less than smooth opening. 'Thanks.'

Craig shot his buddy a look and rolled his eyes. His gaze settled on me, and he offered a boyish grin. 'Look, Brooke, we were wondering if maybe we could go beyond the teasing and make this a real thing tonight. Maybe we could come inside and show you how much we appreciate those performances.'

'Oh.' I didn't know what to say. The fantasy I'd craved had just popped up on my doorstep. Was I really interested in making it reality? Or was this something best left in the realm of make-believe? 'I'm not sure.'

'We don't want to pressure you,' Jay said quickly. 'It's just that we've been watching you from the beginning, and you're so damn hot and so much fun. We've always had a threesome on our bucket list and then tonight you put on that crazy show. It just seemed like fate.'

Craig shrugged. 'We thought it wouldn't hurt to ask.'

'Well,' I said, wavering with indecision. 'I don't know. I mean, that's just a game to me.' I gestured toward the glass door leading out to my balcony. 'It's not supposed to be an advertisement.'

'Maybe not, but you make bad look so good, baby,' Jay replied, his voice husky.

My tummy flip-flopped at his tone. I looked from man to man and realized I'd be an idiot to send them away. Ridiculously sexy, hot-as-hell men weren't exactly beating down my door every night. I hadn't slept with a real man in nearly five months, and here were two perfect specimens of manhood begging me to let them into my bed.

I stepped aside and gestured toward my living room. 'Come inside.'

Their faces lit up with broad grins at my invitation. When they walked past, I caught the scents of their colognes. Unlike so many men my age, they didn't douse themselves in it but had applied just enough to tantalize me.

I'd no sooner locked the door and turned around to face them before Craig was cupping my face and claiming my mouth in an insistent kiss. I relaxed into his searching tongue and slid my arms around his waist as he backed me up against Jay's chest. Sandwiched between the pair of friends, I let whatever inhibitions I still possessed fade away. I chose to surrender completely to this experience.

Jay pulled the kimono from my shoulders and let it drop to the floor between our feet as Craig continued to kiss me. Jay's hands spanned my belly and glided up toward my breasts. I broke away from Craig's mouth and gasped. Jay murmured his apologies against my neck as he kneaded my tender breasts. Craig's lips found mine again, and he assuaged the pain with his skillful mouth.

Soon we found our way to the couch. My babydoll disappeared with one swift yank, and I was pulled down on to Craig's lap, my thighs resting atop his. Jay knelt between my knees and grasped my waist as he lowered his mouth to my clit. I cried out with pleasure at the touch of his tongue and soft lips. He proved his skill in eating pussy. I held tight to Craig's wrists as Jay lapped at my honeyed cunt and pushed me closer and closer to climax. 'Oh! Oh! Ah! Unnhh!'

Bliss burst in my belly and rocketed through my chest. My entire body buzzed as Jay went wild between my thighs, his tongue flicking and circling until I begged him to stop, to show mercy. He sat back, smiling like the Cheshire cat, and wiped his mouth on the back of his hand. Craig turned my face until our mouths met. I was vaguely aware of the sounds of Jay stripping out of his clothing.

I stiffened with surprise when Jay scooped me right

up out of Craig's arms. He nuzzled my neck and nipped at my earlobe. 'Where is your bedroom?'

'That way.' Still breathless, I pointed toward the hall. 'Last room at the end.'

Jay hustled toward my bedroom, Craig close on his heels. There was some fumbling as Craig tried to find the switch on the lamp next to my bed. When the room was illuminated, Jay embraced his inner caveman and tossed me on to the bed. I laughed and crooked my finger, beckoning the pair of them to join me atop the mattress. Jay crawled over me and smothered me with deep kisses as Craig hastily shucked his clothing. I heard the unmistakable crinkle of condom wrappers as he slipped out of his jeans and assumed Craig had brought protection with him. I liked a man who was prepared!

The bed dipped again, alerting me to Craig's presence. I relished the erotic sensations of both men kissing and licking and nibbling my body. Two mouths teased my breasts. Ten fingers slid between my thighs and explored the wet depths of my cunt. I closed my eyes and reveled in the debauchery of being their plaything. No fantasy could compete with the reality of a threesome.

'Are you ready, honey?' Jay's questioning gaze met mine.

I nodded and laughed. 'As I'll ever be.'

Craig pecked my cheek and rolled away just long enough to put on a condom. Jay caressed my face and kissed me until my head swam. 'You're so beautiful,' he whispered against my mouth.

My heart melted as his fingertips trailed along my cheek. Jay seemed a bit more invested in our tryst than Craig, and I wondered if maybe, just maybe, this night would lead to the possibility of a new relationship.

Craig's hand stroked my shoulder, and I turned to face him. As I crawled on to his lap and straddled his thighs, Jay hopped off the bed and disappeared from the bedroom. I figured he'd gone in search of the lube and let it go. Besides, the pulling sensation of Craig's mouth wrapped around my nipple made my clit throb almost painfully. I was soaking wet and dripping on to him. I needed that long ruddy cock of his deep inside my pussy. Like, right now.

I grasped Craig's dick and guided him into position. With one hard thrust, he slid home. We both groaned and clutched at one another. I was starting to build up a nice rhythm, gyrating like a belly dancer atop his hips, when Jay reappeared and climbed up on to the bed behind me. He cupped my breast with one hand as the fingers of the other penetrated my ass.

In no time at all, I was begging him to take me, to shove his cock deep in my backside. Jay happily obliged, his fat cock impaling me with a slow, steady thrust that knocked the air from my lungs. Grinning mischievously, I planted my hands on Craig's chest and got ready for the ride of my young life. We laughed as we tried to figure out the perfect tempo.

Soon, we'd mastered the art of double penetration and were rocking and bucking ourselves toward mind-blowing climaxes. I shrieked like a banshee when my orgasm consumed me. I couldn't think, couldn't breathe and couldn't speak. All I could do was come, come so hard I thought I might die from the sheer exquisite bliss of the moment.

As we clung together in a sweaty heap of spent bodies, I decided that fake double dildo of mine was going in the trash. After this wild night, I'd finally had a taste of the real thing, and no cheap imitation would ever satisfy me. I'd graduated to a whole new plane of sexual existence, and I was never going back.

The Shop
Lisette Ashton

I work in a sex shop and, I have to admit, the job does have a lot of perks.

I got my job at The Shop through a friend of a friend. I don't think anyone ever starts working in a sex shop because it's a legitimate career choice. Or because they've applied through the normal channels that result in an applicant being offered a position. I think it's always a case of the recommendation of a friend of a friend.

Ted knew I was looking for work. Richard told Ted that he had a vacancy at The Shop. Ted must have remembered the wrist-job I gave him the previous evening as a forfeit for a drinking game. And, consequently, Ted put my name forward and orchestrated an introduction.

Richard had reservations. 'Women can put punters off,' he explained.

'I guess that's possible,' I agreed. 'But isn't it also likely a woman behind the counter might help improve sales?'

I started arguing about how it might make the shop more accessible to female customers, opening his market to an untapped fifty per cent share of the population. I started trying to tell Richard that his core client base of male customers might be more interested in obtaining a female perspective on the suitability of their purchases. He silenced me with a wave of his hand and told me I was talking too much sales bullshit. He said I didn't know what the hell I was talking about. But he said he'd trial me with a three-month probation.

He said then that there were lots of perks to working in a sex shop. But, before he could explain what those perks were, he went strangely solemn and said, 'There's just one rule while you're working in the shop.'

He spoke in such a peculiar fashion that I fell silent. It sounded like the moment when Bluebeard tells his new wife that she must never try to open the locked door to the seventh room. I urged Richard to continue.

'You must never have sex with a customer for money.'

I should have balked. I should have told Richard that I didn't have sex with *anyone* for money, let alone his grubby little customers in his seedy little shop. What the hell did he think I was? Instead, because I needed the job, I simply told him I would obey that rule.

It never occurred to me that it would be a difficult rule to obey.

All of which is how I ended up spending my evenings surrounded by the town's largest selection of vibrators and a world-class collection of pornographic magazines and DVDs. I sat behind the counter from noon until ten o'clock at night. I was trying to look efficient but approachable. And I smiled for the steady supply of male customers who scurried furtively through the shop desperate to make their quick and anonymous purchases.

To my surprise, I discovered it was quite an arousing atmosphere.

There were dirty films constantly being played in the background.

Erotic films.

Pornographic movies.

Because I was expected to pick the films that were played, the movies were always those that I wanted to see. In the first few weeks my choices were fairly vanilla. I picked up the *Horny Housewife* films and the *Adventurous Amateur* titles. This changed to a broader interest as I experimented with various genres of movie. In later months I found I was picking some of the most depraved titles from the stockroom and happily enjoying them again and again. *Whipping Girl* remains one of my favourite films. Watching the hero slash a strap across that woman's backside and seeing her cheeks marked with red stripes …

But I digress.

It's enough to say that there's something highly arousing about the sound of fake orgasms being repeated through every working hour of the day. Hearing that soundtrack is definitely one of the perks. And, while it might sound like an arrogant claim, I believe my experience in the shop has allowed me to become enough of a connoisseur to differentiate between the sound of fake orgasms and the sound of real ones.

I could try to be coy and prim and proper and pretend that I was never really affected by the noise. But the truth is it got me warm and moist and horny.

And that was just the background noise.

The magazines were even more stimulating.

Part of my duties involved making sure the magazines were displayed neatly. The shocking cover images startled me at first. They showed strikingly attractive women impaled on impossibly huge erections. They showed scenes of anal sex and lesbian sex and group sex. They were graphically illustrated with hundreds of glossy images. Every picture showed a sexual act recreated in rich and glorious detail.

I borrowed a copy of *Pussy Hungry* from the shelves and took it back to the counter. Marvelling at the pictures of female mouths devouring female genitals, I worked my way through it from cover to cover. By the time I had finished I was sitting in a puddle of my own arousal. The muscles of my sex were a cramp-like pain of unsatisfied frustration and need.

Two weeks into the job and I was masturbating while I sat at the till.

There was no one in the shop.

Behind me I could hear the sounds of a high-pitched bottle-blonde bimbo screeching her way to a fake climax. This was one of the main stars from *Naughty Neighbours XIII*, one of those vanilla films I favoured during my first weeks in the shop. And I was reading my way through a filthy story about a woman being spit-roasted in a magazine entitled *3-Way*.

I was so horny my pussy muscles were clenching and convulsing in pre-orgasmic spasms. My pants felt as though they had stuck to the wet lips of my labia. I could drink in the gamey scent of my arousal with every breath. And I was desperate to suffer the release of a climax. The need had come over me like a compulsion. I had a desperate yearning to exorcise the arousal from my body.

I was wearing jeans.

A part of me wanted to scrabble with the belt – unfasten that. Scrabble with the buttons – unfasten those. Scrabble with the zip – and then tug the jeans down to my hips so I had unfettered access to myself. But I didn't have the time or the patience. The need within me was an urgent one and I had no desire to be sat with my jeans and panties wrenched down to my thighs while I frigged myself to an awkward and uncomfortable climax.

I parted my thighs and pushed my fist between my legs. I pressed it hard against the seat of the chair. The base of my thumb jutted towards me and I rubbed myself against it. It only took a roll of my hips, a roll as though I was riding against a broad and rigid cock, and the first tremors of a climax began to shiver through my body. As soon as I realised what I was doing, as soon as I privately acknowledged that I was wanking in the shop, the excitement grew even more intense.

It was behaviour as bold as exhibitionism or outdoor sex. It was behaviour as depraved as anything I had ever done in my life – and no one had ever called me a prude when it came to sex – and it was totally exhilarating.

I rocked my hips slowly back and forth.

The seam at the crotch of my jeans was a rock-hard ridge that pressed against my clitoris. The sensation dithered between an absolute agony and a furious, satisfying delight. Grinding harder and faster against my own wrist and the seam of the jeans, I rubbed myself to a slow and deliberate climax.

The explosion began in the tips of my toes. It was a tingle of pure pleasure that trembled through my legs and caused the muscles in my thighs to spasm. It travelled up to the centre of my sex and culminated in a warm wet eruption between my thighs. I stifled a groan of satisfaction and allowed the ripples of pleasure to eddy through my body.

I was still shivering when the shop's bell rang and a customer walked in.

I blushed, as though he could have known what I'd been doing. My heart hammered. Each pounding beat made me feel as though I'd been caught in the act. I imagined that I looked dishevelled and ravaged, although the truth was that I probably had a little colour in my cheeks and no other obvious symptoms of satisfaction. Nevertheless, we studied one another until the customer rushed out of the shop without making a purchase.

And I told myself I would never do it again.

Jilling myself in the job had been too risky and I couldn't face the embarrassment or the consequences of being caught doing something so depraved. And yet, while those arguments made sense, the next morning I dressed in a skirt rather than jeans.

I didn't even realise why I'd made such a fashion choice until I was browsing through another of the magazines that I happened to have pulled from the shelves: *Back Door Sluts*.

This was a magazine about anal sex.

It showed glossy pictures of feminine backsides being spread by thick throbbing cocks. Some of the pictures showed dual penetration. Two massive cocks slid side by side into one woman. Those pictures left me breathless

24

with a hungry desire to be the woman in the picture. I could imagine myself being the subject of so much hot, sweaty intimacy. The thought had me close to melting.

I glanced towards the shop's collection of vibrators with an avaricious eye.

It was the largest selection of dildos and plastic cocks that I had ever seen. I wasn't even sure where my thoughts were going as I studied them, except for the fact that I was thinking about the perks of the job. I was close to doubling over with a violent sexual need.

I teased a hand against my bare thigh.

That was all that was needed to have me desperate for more.

Within a moment my hand had slipped beneath the hem of my skirt. I tugged the sopping crotch of my panties to one side. And then I was caressing the moist split of my sex and was only seconds away from climaxing.

Wearing a skirt made it easier to bring myself off.

I could draw slow and lazy circles against the thrust of my clitoris. I could slide one finger, and then two, in and out of the warm, syrupy heat of my pussy. Wearing a skirt made it simple for me to squeeze the bud of my clitoris and wring a searing climax from its centre.

I came with a growl of bitter satisfaction.

Maddeningly, after a week, I realised that I needed more.

I took a modest-sized vibrator from the shelves. By

a stroke of unprecedented good fortune, I happened to have brought a pair of batteries into the shop with me that day. I think it was the same subconscious stroke of unprecedented good fortune that had me wearing skirts to work each morning. The batteries fitted into the vibrator. Within seconds it was buzzing brightly in my hands. I covered it with a condom and then slipped it inside my pussy.

I was so wet there was no resistance. The buzzing length of plastic simply pushed its way into my cunt.

I almost climaxed from the thrill of that sensation alone. And I held my breath for a moment, savouring the dizzying rush of pleasure that came from the throbbing and pulsing sensations that shot through my pussy.

By the end of that day, I was weak-kneed from suffering multiple climaxes. That was one hell of a perk.

By the end of the month, I had acquired a collection of different-sized vibrators and dildos and plugs from the shop's shelves. Sometimes I would use two at the same time. I'd have a plug nestled inside my anus and a dithering vibrator throbbing through my pussy. I tried to imagine what it would be like to serve a customer while those delicious sensations were pounding through me. The idea was so exciting it always brought me to a shuddering explosion of pleasure. I could picture myself struggling to appear calm and unaffected on the exterior while creaming myself internally. The idea was so stimulating I would explode as soon as the image filled my thoughts.

And, when I first did manage to serve a customer while impaled on two plastic cocks, I only just managed to hold back my screams of euphoria.

It went on for a month before I got caught.

Richard paid an unexpected visit to the shop.

He came in while I was frigging myself to a slow climax over the pages of *No Holes Barred*. Fortunately I wasn't using any of the plugs or dildos that day. I had only slipped my moist and eager fingers against the slippery folds of my sex. I tried to pretend I wasn't doing anything. I tried to casually slip my hand away from beneath my skirt but he gave me an understanding wink.

'This place gets everyone like that,' he assured me. As an afterthought he added, 'Just make sure you never have sex with a customer for money.'

I heard the words.

But this time they didn't make me as angry as they had on that first day.

'Do you really think I'm likely to do that?' I asked.

He shrugged. 'If one of the punters catches you wanking he'll likely make an offer. And I realise that I'm only just paying minimum wage, so I don't doubt you'll be tempted. But I can't let you carry on working here if I catch you doing that.'

He went on to explain that it could mean he'd lose

his licence as an adult bookseller, and that a store clerk whoring herself to the punters was likely to cut into his profits. He went on to point out that there was a noticeboard of business cards behind the till, each one advertising the services of someone local who was willing to exchange sex for cash.

I'd seen the noticeboard on previous occasions and had marvelled at the number of exotic names on there, but I didn't have time to discuss it with Richard. I was busy assuring him that I had no intention of fucking anyone for money. And I wanted him to hurry out of the shop so I could finish rubbing myself to climax.

He had an erection, I noticed.

It jutted at the front of his pants and I guessed it had come about because he had seen me rubbing myself off. He asked what magazine I'd been reading and, when I showed him *No Holes Barred*, I noticed his erection grew more pronounced. The temptation to reach out and stroke his hard-on was almost irresistible. He was standing so close I wouldn't have had to stretch to touch the bulge at the front of his pants and slide my hand up and down him.

And, from what I could see, he looked to have a decent size on him. He wasn't as well built as the men in the magazines I'd been reading, or the ones in the films that I'd been watching. But he looked to have large enough equipment to satisfy. And I was thinking about his equipment when he left the shop. As soon as he was out of the door I rubbed myself to a delicious climax.

And, in the embarrassed aftermath, I vowed that I wouldn't get into the habit of wanking while I was at work. I should have been mortified that my boss had caught me with my fingers inside my own honey-pot. The fact that I was untroubled by the encounter made me wonder what sort of depraved slut I had become.

The next day I wore a shorter skirt.

I found myself a copy of *Cock Addict*.

And that was the day when I got caught wanking by one of the customers.

I was busy rubbing myself to a leisurely climax when the bell went. There was a butt-plug inside my anus but I hadn't got round to pressing a vibrator into my cunt. After lubricating the butt-plug and easing it into place, I had only been able to slide my lube-smeared fingers against the greasy lips of my sex. And, when the bell over the door jangled to announce a customer, I figured it was time for me to have some proper fun.

At first I thought it would be Richard again.

I was curious to know how he would react to me wanking him to a climax while I rubbed myself off. Since he'd caught me the previous day, and raised no objections to my indiscretion, I thought I could carry on. I could maybe greet him with a cheeky opening like, 'Thank God you're here. I've been desperate for some cock all morning.'

But this customer was a stranger – someone I'd never seen before.

He cast a furtive glance towards me.

I stared boldly back at him. I was in a zone of arousal where nothing mattered other than my satisfaction. I raised a glistening finger to my lips and then licked it slowly. My tongue traced the tip of the nail. Then I enveloped the finger with my mouth, sucking it as though it was a cock.

Mesmerised, the customer simply stared.

I let the finger move from my mouth and then slipped it down between my legs. The customer couldn't see what was going on. The counter spoiled his view. But I have no doubt his imagination was furnishing him with every horny detail of my finger stroking at the wet lips of my pussy.

I never broke eye contact with him. All the time that he stood in the doorway, I stared at him with a passion and intensity that left him in no doubt that I was enjoying a rush of personal pleasure.

In my mind's eye I was naked with him and we were both alone and savouring the satisfying tease of my fingers on my cunt. I moved the finger away. I beckoned him to approach. And then I licked my pussy juices from the knuckle.

He walked closer to the counter.

I lowered the finger back to my wetness.

When he was close enough I pulled back the hem of my skirt so he could see what I was doing. The dark bush of my pubes devoured the tips of my fingers. The rich scent of my sex filled the shop. The squelch of two fingers sliding in and out of my sex was almost as loud as the background noise of porn-movie soundtrack.

The customer sighed.

I could see the thrust of the erection inside his pants. It was satisfying to think I had been the cause of his excitement. I began to rub myself with even more ferocity as I realised how much he wanted me.

He reached out a hand, as though he was going to caress my thigh.

And then he seemed to think better of it.

I came with a barely muted shriek of satisfaction. I clutched at the counter with my one free hand. My vision misted crimson as the rush of pleasure flooded through me.

The customer's erection throbbed inside his pants.

Almost immediately a black patch of wetness stained the front of his jeans. His mouth fell open in a small O of surprise. And then it broke into a grin as he appraised me with a newfound respect.

'That was one of the horniest things I've ever seen in my life,' the customer told me. He slammed down two ten-pound notes on the counter and headed for the door.

'What's that for?' I asked.

'My way of saying thank you,' he said. Then the bell was jangling behind him.

31

And, while I knew it couldn't technically be described as exchanging sex for money, when I picked up the notes and stuffed them into my purse, I realised I was running the risk of breaking Richard's one rule of employment.

The next day I didn't bother wearing panties.

I didn't even need a magazine, although I found a copy of *Wet* and began to work my way through the pages. When Richard came in and found me masturbating, I didn't even bother stopping.

'You're enjoying your work here,' he observed wryly.

'Get over here. Get your cock out.' I was at that delicious stage of arousal where I could only spit the words. The ferocity of my passion had transformed my speech into insistent grunts.

Obligingly, Richard walked over to the counter where I stood. He didn't get his cock out but he made no objection when I tugged down the zip on his jeans and then extricated his length through the gaping hole of the fly.

His flesh was violently warm. When my fingers touched him I could feel the throbbing pulse of his excitement beneath the steely surface of his erection.

'Jesus,' Richard muttered. 'I didn't expect this.'

I said nothing. I squeezed my clit. I continued to rub the hyper-sensitive surface and then slip a finger in and out between my oily lips. And I rolled my other fist back and forth along the length of his cock.

It was as satisfying as I'd expected. His size was larger than average, but not as daunting as those featured in the magazines and DVDs I'd been watching. I could imagine him filling me easily and completely if he bent me over the counter and decided to ride me until I screamed through an orgasm.

That thought was pushing me towards the brink of a climax when the bell over the shop's door rang.

The customer who had watched me the day before stood in the doorway. He saw that I was tugging at Richard's cock and he smiled tightly.

I gave him a heavy wink and then blew him a kiss.

It was all that he needed.

He looked set to say something, and then he drew a deep breath. I saw him stare down at his pants as another dark stain began to spread across the front. He glanced up at me and shook his head in rueful disbelief.

As I continued to stroke my fist back and forth along Richard's cock, the customer slammed two tens on the counter.

'It's worth coming in here just to see you,' he told me.

And then the bell was jangling behind him.

'I thought I told you not to have sex with the customers,' Richard growled.

His cock remained rigid. The single eye stared at me with blind fury. I tightened my grip around him and continued to stroke slowly back and forth.

'It's not really having sex with customers if they just see me wanking, is it?'

Richard looked set to argue the point.

I moved my lips around his cock and sucked lightly on the end of his shaft. He tasted of sweet saltiness. The flavour made my cunt clutch greedily around my fingers. Eventually, I moved my lips away.

'Give me a second chance,' I urged. 'And I'll make sure you get greeted like this every day that I'm working here.'

He groaned. 'You drive a hard bargain,' he murmured. 'But, under the arrangement you've just suggested, I'm prepared to overlook the matter this once.'

I took his cock into my mouth and nodded. And swallowed.

* * *

That was three years ago and I've been working here ever since.

As I say, the job has a lot of perks. Seeing Richard every other day is only one of them. Welcoming a steady clientele of customers who are happy to pay good money for the pleasure of watching me play with myself is another perk. Of course, I know I can't stay in this job forever. But I'm determined to stay in this position until something better comes along. And, if anything better ever does come my way, you'll be the first to find out.

Come In Handy
Heather Towne

I lusted after Carrie from the moment I set eyes on her. She was playing tennis by herself – smacking a fuzzy yellow ball against the side of the school building – dressed in a pair of white short-shorts and a white tank-top. Her limbs gleamed long and lean and smooth, sunbrowned, her yellow-blonde hair braided back in a ponytail, a white sun visor on her head. She had green eyes and a pretty oval face, with plush lips.

I was just walking past the school and the tennis courts on my way to the convenience store, when I saw the vision of loveliness, and I stopped in my tracks and stared. I'd just come off my first full-out lesbian experience with a cousin of mine, and I was hooked on girls, anxious to hook up again with a member of my own sexy sex. So I stood and watched Carrie whack the ball off the wall, marveling at the way the long muscles on her arms and legs rippled, the way her breasts bounced up and down.

'Hey, do you play?' she suddenly called out, catching the ball and looking my way.

I went on gaping.

'Um, I was wondering if you –'

'Sure! I play!' I yelped, giving my head a shake. She wanted me to 'play' with her. I ran over as fast as my shapely little legs could carry me.

'I'm Carrie,' she said in a voice of milk and honey, sticking out a hand. 'I guess my friend's not showing up, so I have no one to play with. I have an extra racquet if you wouldn't mind …'

I grabbed on to her slender brown hand and squeezed it. 'I'd love to play with you!' I gushed. Her hand was warm and soft. 'I'm Tina!'

She bent down and plucked out the other tennis racquet from her bag. I was enthralled by the long sleek lines of the girl, the breathtaking glimpse of cleavage. She straightened up and handed me the racquet.

'Shall we?' she said, indicating with a sweep of her arm the tennis courts behind her.

'We shall indeed,' I breathed.

Tennis isn't really my game. But I did my best, chasing down balls and swatting them back into the net, sometimes over. Carrie had me running all over the place, ducking her spikes and serves. By the end of the first set I was sweating with more than exertion under the hot sun. The sight of Carrie stretching and straining, running, leaping up and leaning into a serve, the sound of her high-pitched grunting and groaning, had me bathed in perspiration more than just weather-related. I took a few balls off the body and head, when I didn't keep my eyes on the fuzzy sphere, too busy ogling its mistress.

She jogged up to the net, racquet and towel and water bottle in hand. She tossed the towel at me, then tilted her long neck back and squirted water down her silken throat. I wiped off my sweating face, keeping my eyes free to see.

'Wanna drink?' she asked after swallowing beautifully.

I swallowed dry. 'Sure.'

She squirted me right in the face.

'Hey!'

'Sorry, just couldn't resist,' she said, laughing. She handed me the water bottle, then plucked the towel out of my hand and proceeded to dry off my moistened face.

My body burned even hotter, the girl crowding closer to me, pushing against the net. She patted down my flushed face, moved the towel lower, on to my flushed chest.

I was wearing just a tank-top and shorts like she was. And as she rubbed over the top of my chest, the long nipples on my little boobs sproinged out even longer, almost piercing my top with desire. I squirted water on my chin, missing my mouth, maybe accidentally, maybe deliberately. Forcing Carrie to keep toweling, caressing.

When the fluffy white cloth brushed over my stiffened buds, propelled by the girl's graceful hands, I couldn't help but gasp. My nipples are as sensitive as my feelings, as easily aroused.

'Whoops, sorry!' Carrie said. 'Shall we get back to the game?'

My legs would barely carry me back to the baseline, they were so weak.

It took the tennis goddess only about another half-hour to polish me off three sets to love.

'Why don't we go back to my place?' she suggested, after nailing down the last spike to put my game out of its misery. 'You can have a cold drink, or grab a shower, if you want. My parents are away for the weekend.'

I bobbed my head, then trailed after Carrie's lithesome legs to her car, keeping an eye on her sweet twitching butt cheeks. Her car was an old beater as befitted an eighteen-year-old. I gratefully climbed in and she cranked up the gusty a/c. We shared some of our life stories as she drove us to her parents' neat little white bungalow ten blocks over.

'I'm going to take a shower. Help yourself to anything in the fridge.' She threw her racquet on to the living-room couch and skipped off down the hall, peeling off her tank-top.

I had a glimpse of bare bronzed, supple-muscled back, before Carrie jumped into the bathroom and closed the door. I staggered into the kitchen, poured myself an ice-cold glass of water that did nothing to cool me down as I chugged.

I placed the empty glass on the counter, then walked down the hallway, up to the bathroom door. I could hear the hiss of hot water, maybe the sound of someone scrubbing their hot naked body. I put a shaky hand against the woodwork. I had to go in, take the plunge.

I dropped my hand down on to the doorknob, gripped it, turned it, pushed the door open a crack. Hot steam billowed into my eyes and nose, as I thrust the peeking face-parts into the opening.

There was a glass partition that rose up from the lip of the bathtub, hiding the sexy shower participant within. Or almost hiding her. The glass was fogged, but I could still clearly see Carrie's long, lean naked outline, the sensuous form of her golden-brown body. I swallowed humid air in a gasp and pushed the bathroom door open further, just enough gap to allow me to slip inside the heated, cloudy haven with the honey.

The glass went almost all the way up to the ceiling, so Carrie couldn't see me through her side of the dewed pane. But I could see her, tilting her head back and letting the needles of soothing, singeing water splash against her chest, spray all over her breasts. There wasn't a tanline anywhere, just delicious, sunkissed babe from head to toe. I moved closer, licking my lips, the glistening girl in the glass cage drawing me like a beacon.

I stopped when she suddenly started humming. She was rubbing soap on to her chest now, a pink bar that she smoothed over and under her firm breasts, circled around the twin pointing, tan tips. I stared like a star-struck tennis fan meeting her racquet idol, following Carrie's every stroking motion in the tub.

Her tank-top and short-shorts were half hanging out of the laundry hamper. I stretched out a hand and grabbed on to her discarded game gear, clutched the bits of cloth to my chest, then my face, watching while the girl sudsed up her jutting breasts.

The soft white cotton tennis togs were drenched in her perfume and perspiration. I pressed them to my nose and mouth, inhaling deeply, gazing at the girl buffing her bod in the shower. My face and body surged with heat, the billowing clouds of steam carrying me away. I rubbed the dampened clothing all over my face, my cheeks, nose, lips, and I shivered, despite the heat.

Clenching the clothing to my face with my left hand, I slid my right downward, on to my breasts. My knees buckled, as my quivering fingers tripped my stiffened nipples, sending shockwaves singing through my body. I strummed the stuck-out pair of shimmering buds, then washed the palm of my hand all around my buzzing breasts, emulating sweet Carrie caressing her golden body in the steamy dunk tank. She had all the right equipment, and skills, for this game, too, and I just couldn't let the opportunity pass without applauding her talents.

She turned around and let the water splash against her curved back, rubbing the bar of soap over her burgeoned, bouncy butt cheeks. My own hand shot around behind me, on to my bum. I rubbed the cheeky pair, breathing Carrie's clothes and essence, staring at the shining girl stripped down to her bare essentials. She slid the soap in between her buttocks and scrubbed, and my hand gripped one of my trembling cheeks, fingernails biting in like my teeth into the sporty girl's top and bottom.

Carrie spun back around in the shower and soaped her long legs. I took the chance of scrabbling my shorts open, shooing them down my legs, baring my beating pussy. My dark trimmed fur was matted with moisture, slit tingling out in the open, in front of the bathing nude hottie.

Carrie's hands slid back up on to her chest. I glided my hand back on to my tits, caressing, clasping, choking. And then the soap and her hand dived down her slender body, over her flat tummy, in between her legs. She rubbed her pussy, shuddering slightly, so it seemed to my shaky vision. My hand jumped off my tits and over my stomach and on to my equally bare, almost equally wet pussy.

'Ohmigod!' I yipped, jerking with the raw sexual impact of my fingers on my pleasure mound.

Carrie's clothes muffled my moan for the most part. She

cocked her head, then went back to rubbing – her pussy.

I balled up her top and shorts and stuffed them right into my mouth, started stroking my pussy. My whole body vibrated with emotion, my cunt a sodden, shimmering mess under my fingers, surging and swimming with passion. I rubbed my engorged lips, buffed my swollen clit, matching Carrie's rapid, pussy-happy movements.

And she was rubbing that soap in between her legs with a little more than just cleanliness in mind. In fact, the girl was getting downright dirty, her left hand sliding up her body and up and under a water-beaded breast, clutching and squeezing the luscious, curved, taut-tipped hunk of feminine flesh. She was feeling herself up, no doubt about it. As I felt myself up.

The steam-heat had gotten to her. I knew the luxuriant feeling well, had wetted my own tub bottom with pussy juice on many an arousing occasion. But never with someone watching me, rubbing herself off to me.

Carrie was oblivious to my breathless excitement right outside her glass door, however. She squeezed her left breast, slid her long silky fingers out to the tip and pinched and rolled her needful nipple; rubbing that lucky pink cake of soap up and down her water-washed muff. I yanked the girl's clothing out of my mouth and rubbed the mouth- and body-moistened cotton all over my heaving chest, churning up even more feeling in my brimming breasts and nipples. As I rubbed harder and faster on my pussy, polishing my button with a passion.

Carrie's beautiful body bowed, the passion seizing her. She clenched her breasts, clawed at her nipples, rubbing and rubbing her pussy so that soap bubbles billowed and burst. She was dripping with more than just water now, I could tell.

I felt her joy, and used it, fondling my own tits and pussy in a frenzy. I was on the slippery edge, primed and ready to go off, clit and nipples pounding with impending explosion. My glaring eyes bleared with the wicked sight of my tennis mate playing her perfect body to perfection.

But then Carrie suddenly put the brakes on her head-long rush to self-ecstasy, sidelined her scintillating sexual game. She went back to bathing.

But she was still baiting – me. I couldn't, wouldn't stop. I dropped her togs and stuffed my hand up my top, grabbing on to a bare breast and squeezing, kneading, furiously petting my pussy down below. I was too far gone to call it quits; this match was going to end on a high note.

I squealed, orgasm bursting out under my fingers and blasting through my body. My clit pumped out pure ecstasy, blazed my being full of it.

I clutched a tit so hard I thought I'd shoot a nipple at Carrie, wave after wave of utter bliss tidal waving through my rippling form. It was silent, sinful, sensational. My mouth gaped open and my eyes bugged out, my body and brain jolted with ultimate joy, repeatedly.

I almost fainted under the sensory onslaught. But I fought to keep my fluttering eyelids open – to focus on water nymph Carrie burnishing her beautiful body.

Somehow, I managed to pull up my shorts and stagger out of the sex room, still shivering with the aftershocks of what I'd seen and felt so deeply. I stumbled back into the hallway, and softly and gratefully shut the bathroom door on that awesome exhibition of eroticism.

And then I saw the open door on my left: Carrie's bedroom. Naughtiness and curiosity re-flooded my excited little form. I walked into her room.

There was a bed, a desk, a chair, a bureau and a dresser. Everything was done up in pink and light blue, fluffy and flouncy. Carrie was obviously a girly-girl, despite her wicked backhand and forehand. I made a beeline for the bureau, knowing just what I was looking for.

I found the treasure trove in the top drawer – the girl's underthingies, panties and bras and stockings and slips. I cocked my head, heard the shower still running full-blast. So I plunged my arms into the slinky underwear, scooping some up and against my face, burying my nose and mouth in the silky soft stuff.

It was wonderful! I inhaled deeply, the scent sweet and clean as the girl herself. There was silk and satin and nylon and spandex, rubbing against my face, all over my face. I stuck out my tongue and swirled it all over the intimate material, opened my mouth and chewed, bathing my beaming face in Carrie's underwear. Until I got an even wickeder, bolder idea.

It took me about ten seconds to shed my top and shorts, leaving them puddled on the blue carpet. It took me about a full minute to slide on a pair of Carrie's pink satin panties, clasp on one of her white Lycra-spandex bras. They were a tad large, but, in my addled mind, a perfect, sensuous fit.

I lurched over to the full-length mirror on the wall and stared at myself. There were goose bumps coating my pale skin, my short black hair almost standing on end. I rubbed out the goose bumps, roaming my hands all over my body, my breasts in Carrie's bra, my pussy in her panties. I sighed with sublime pleasure, as I caressed my cunt through the satin, squeezed my breasts through the spandex.

I was rubbing faster, groping harder, lost in the lust of it all, rushing toward wanton self-fulfillment in another girl's bedroom and duds. When the shower suddenly switched off and the water stopped running.

I just barely had Carrie's underthings squared back away and my own clothes back on, when the girl stepped out of the bathroom and into the bedroom wrapped up in a towel.

'Did you get yourself something to drink?'

'Y-yeah. Something to drink.'

Her shoulders shone buff and brown, her blonde hair streaming loose down her back now, long legs spilling golden out of the bottom of the towel, feet slender and shapely as the rest of her. 'I'm just going to change. If you want to use the shower, go right ahead.'

'Huh? No, no. I, uh, think I'll get another drink. I could use one.'

I ran down the hall to the kitchen, poured myself another cold one and tossed it down. It didn't quench the raging fire in my body one bit.

But it did make me want to pee.

Carrie's bedroom door was cracked open an inch or so. I just had to peek inside.

I was rocked back on my heels by what I saw.

The girl was stretched out on her bed, back to the headboard, long legs out and apart. She was totally naked. She had one hand on her pussy, rubbing, her other hand cupping a tit, squeezing.

I couldn't breathe. My eyes swelled so wide they almost popped right out of my head.

The girl was absolutely gorgeous in full living color, with no glass separating us, a vision of golden-brown smooth feminine loveliness, engaged in that most intimate of female behaviors. She moaned softly, biting her lip, as she rubbed her strip-shaved pussy, clutched her B-cup breasts. I bit my lip and moaned right along, drinking in the intoxicating scene and getting dizzy all over again.

'I always like to relax after a match,' someone said. 'After getting so worked up.'

That was Carrie speaking – to me. She was looking at me gawking at her from the doorway, not the least bit self-conscious, apparently.

I, on the other hand, was barely conscious, as I slipped inside her bedroom and stumbled over to her bed and sat down next to the naked girl.

'L-let me help you,' someone stammered. Me! 'It's better than playing alone.'

Carrie grinned. 'I never thought of that.'

I looked up into her sparkling green eyes, down at her blonde-dewed pussy. She'd dropped her right hand away from her cunt, and I replaced it with my shaking left hand, reaching out and touching my trembling fingertips to the top of her slit.

'Mmmm!' she murmured, shivering slightly.

She was wet, her pussy lips pink and engorged beneath the blonde fur. I stroked them, brushed them, found her hard, throbbing clit with my fingers and rubbed. She quivered, grasping my other hand and placing it on one of her breasts.

I gasped, and quivered. It'd all happened so fast, was so utterly sensual. Me rubbing a nude girl's pussy in her own bedroom, clasping and kneading her breast.

Carrie's cunt welled even wetter under my rubbing

hand. Her breast filled my other hand, firm and hot and beating with her heart, tan nipple stiffening before my very appreciative eyes. She undulated against my hands, giving up her body to me.

'Stick your fingers inside me! Your entire fist!'

I looked up at her face, my hands freezing on her pussy and boobs. Her eyes were shining. Her chest heaved in my hand, pussy pushing up against my palm. She nodded her head and gripped my wrist, plunging my pointed fingers right into her slit.

'Yes!' she cried, driving my fingers – all five of them – deep inside herself.

I stared down at half of my hand buried in the girl's cunt, hardly believing it, surging with raw emotion like I'd never felt before. I balled my fingers into a fist inside her, and she drove the rest of my hand into her pussy.

Her lips swelled obscenely, swallowing up my left hand. It was wicked, crazy, insanely erotic. I was in up to my wrist in the girl's burning hot wetness. She groaned and gripped my elbow and shoved me in even deeper, halfway up my forearm.

'Oh, Tina! Tina!' she wailed, wallowing on the end of my arm up her cunt.

I didn't know what to do. I'd never done anything like *this* before.

Carrie knew what to do. She pumped my fist and forearm back and forth inside her pussy, fucking herself with my arm. I gripped her tit so hard her nipple almost popped off, holding on for the wild ride.

She bent almost double, glaring at me in the face from inches away, her eyes and mouth wide open, churning my arm in her cunt. This was deeper than I'd ever expected to go with a girl!

Carrie yanked my forearm and fist out of her steaming pussy, both of us gushing with feeling.

'Sorry to be so selfish,' she gasped. She brought my hand up to her mouth and licked off her own sticky juices, swirling her pink tongue all around my shiny, twitching fingers. 'I've got an ... instrument that will get us both into the game.'

'A tennis racquet?' I gulped.

She laughed and leapt off the bed, then ran over to the dresser. She bent down and pulled the bottom drawer open, giving me a jaw-dropping view of her split-peach bottom. She pulled a huge red double-headed jelly dong out of the drawer, then jumped back on to the bed with it.

'Here, take off your clothes.'

I popped my top and skinned down my shorts, quickly getting as nude as she was, almost as lewd. She slid down on to her back on the bed and plowed one bulbous end of the dong into her pussy, deep.

'You've got a lovely body,' she murmured, reaching up and fondling my breasts. My nipples elongated another quarter-inch.

'OK, now you get on the other end, over the top of me.'

She waggled the dong at me, the half that wasn't immersed inside of her. I swallowed, hard. I'd never played this game before, either.

'Come on,' Carrie urged, beckoning with the exposed dong-head.

I climbed over the top of her. She inserted the mushroomed tip into my pussy, pushed it home. I groaned, collapsing on top of the girl. The dong sank deep into my tunnel.

We were together, joined at the sodden cunts by that red jelly two-headed pleasure toy inside us both.

Carrie gripped my bum and pumped her hips. I felt the dong move inside me. Joy rippled my body in waves. I pumped my hips, pleasuring her with the motion. We got a rhythm going, fucking one another, our bodies and pussies melding together.

It was intense, exquisite, awesomely erotic. I stared into Carrie's staring eyes, our hot breath bathing each other's face, hard nipples rubbing together, breasts squishing. We moved faster and faster, fucking with the dong. Until our lust totally erupted.

We screamed, coming, the bed and our bodies bouncing, dong plunging both ends. I shuddered, orgasm exploding in my stuffed and chuffed cunt and pumping through my body. I gushed pure ecstasy, Carrie doing the same. We doused one another with our hot steaming juices.

Afterward, Carrie pushed me aside and jumped up off the bed. 'Nothing like a good workout, after a good workout, I always say,' she said, looking back at me in the mirror, her glorious body glowing.

I smiled at her smiling reflection.

'Let's play again real soon, OK?'

I blissfully nodded. I could always use all the exercise and sexercise I could get. Love, Carrie!

Hard Copy
Elizabeth Coldwell

It's hard to believe now, but I almost didn't go to the office Christmas party. It's not that I'm the antisocial type, but, when you've been part of the workforce as long as I have, you no longer have the same desire to spend an evening standing around with people you don't really like that much, drinking indifferent white wine and listening to the marketing manager doing his oh-so-amusing Sean Connery impression for the thousandth time. Sharing sloppy, open-mouthed kisses with the very married head of the sales department under the mistletoe, letting him grind his cock against me while he took great, groping handfuls of my bum cheeks? Going home with the cute guy in accounts I'd had my eye on since he joined the company, even though I knew it was destined to be nothing more than an unmemorable one-night stand? Oh, yes, I'd done all that, and more, before now. And I had no desire to do it all again.

The last couple of years, I'd found excuses to be somewhere else on the night of the party, and, when the invitations to this year's get-together appeared in my inbox, my initial instinct was to send out an automatic 'sorry, can't make it' in reply. But the more I thought about it, the more I knew I had to make an appearance for once.

Six months ago, the firm who'd employed me for the best part of a decade had been bought out after protracted and unsettling takeover negotiations. Our new CEO, Damon Bennington, was barely out of his twenties, ambitious – and happiest with sycophantic team players around him, particularly those closest to his own age. Rumours of impending redundancies had been sweeping the firm in recent weeks, and I knew that, in my early forties and on the salary package I commanded as a result of so many years' devoted service to my previous company, I'd be a prime candidate for a swift, cost-cutting layoff. Failing to make an appearance at the party might only serve to convince Bennington my face no longer fitted in his set-up, and I couldn't afford the consequences of him reaching that decision. So I bit my lip and RSVP-ed in the affirmative.

***

Looking round the boardroom, which had been made festive for the occasion by tacking a few paper streamers to the ceiling tiles and draping tinsel across the tops of the picture frames, I drained my glass of lukewarm Pinot Grigio and wondered how much longer I'd have to wait it out before I'd done a good enough job of showing my face. It was gone eight o'clock; somehow I'd already managed to waste two hours of my life here. At least this year no one had suggested handing out Secret Santa presents to each other, sparing me the job of choosing a gift for some random member of staff who more than likely wouldn't appreciate whatever I bought them.

Damon and a couple of the boys from the sales department were huddled together in a corner, looking at something on Damon's iPhone and giggling. 'Looks like Chelsea are getting hammered,' I heard Damon mutter with evident satisfaction as I passed them on my way out of the room. From the slight slurring of his voice, I reckoned they weren't the only ones.

Out in the corridor, Julie from sales was showing off her acrylic nail extensions, airbrushed with glittery little snowflakes for the occasion, to a chorus of admiring oohs and ahs. Caring as much about her fashion choices as I did about the evening's football scores, I decided it was time to make a move. Everyone was wrapped up in their own little cliques and conversations; I wouldn't be missed. I'd had a few words with Damon early in the evening, before the drink really kicked in, thanking him for throwing the party and leaving a lipsticked kiss on his cheek. Like a master criminal lining up an alibi, I'd made sure he would remember my having been in the boardroom, even if he couldn't say with any certainty for how long.

The company's premises sprawled across two floors of a nondescript low-rise block. One floor down from the boardroom was my office, where I'd left my coat; I took the back stairs, steel-tipped heels clattering on the treads, and pushed open the fire door that led to the main corridor, anxious to collect my possessions and be away as quickly as I could.

Halfway to my office, my eye was distracted by a flash of light coming from the copy room. The blinds on all the windows had been pulled down, hastily it seemed, as a couple were still open wide enough to let harsh white light spill out as the machine made copy after copy. Despite myself, my interest was piqued; who could still be working at this time of night, and what were they copying that required such secrecy?

Wondering if I was about to stumble on some unheralded act of industrial espionage, I pushed the door open a crack. Whatever I'd expected to see as I peeked into the room, it wasn't the sight that accosted me – a man sitting on the photocopier, trousers and underwear pulled down round his ankles as the machine faithfully reproduced his bare arse time and again.

Until that moment, I'd sworn all the stories I'd heard

of people photocopying their most intimate places were urban myths, nothing more. But the evidence was there before my eyes, slithering out of the copier at a rate of 24 sheets a minute.

Dragging my gaze away from the loosely draped shirt tails that just managed to conceal his cock and balls, I looked up, anxious to see who I'd caught in this outrageous act. It shouldn't have surprised me that the half-naked body before me belonged to Charlie Graves. Damon's closest friend in the company, Charlie held the official title of 'operations manager'. In principle, that seemed to involve loafing around at his desk during working hours, studying figures on the spreadsheets that always seemed to pop up whenever someone passed his desk, disguising the websites he'd been surfing. We all knew his real role within the company was to accompany Damon on long lunches, laugh a little too loudly at his jokes and enthusiastically agree to whatever proposals the CEO put forward for increasing productivity in the office. Strangely, none of those proposals ever seemed to involve removing Charlie from the payroll.

That said, more than a few of the girls who worked in this place would be disappointed if Charlie wasn't around. He might have had all the managerial aptitude of a pot plant, but even I couldn't deny he was very easy on the eye. Six foot or more of muscled perfection – or as perfect as you can find outside the airbrushed abs of the men who model for fitness-magazine covers. His eyes were a striking shade of blue-green that twinkled in his high-cheekboned face, and the ends of his dark carelessly tousled hair rested on the collars of his suit jackets. If that wasn't enough to set most of the female members of staff – and a couple of the male ones, too – drooling whenever he passed, he also had one of the biggest cocks I'd ever seen, at least in its limp state. Charlie was proud of his endowment; he went jogging at lunchtime, making a regular circuit of the docks that stretched away behind our office building, and, when he did, he always wore a pair of tight-fitting Lycra cycling shorts, displaying his dick in almost indecent detail. He wanted us to look, to admire, to covet – and he revelled in the reactions he provoked whenever he strutted into the kitchen to fill his water bottle before setting off on his run.

Certain he hadn't seen me, I looked more closely at him. If it wasn't for those infuriating shirt tails, I'd have the perfect view of his cock, and I prayed for Charlie to shift position, so the limp white cotton would fall to one side and reveal him in all his glory.

Almost as though he'd read my mind, he reached out to adjust the controls on the side of the machine, and, as he did, his thighs slid wider apart, the motion causing the shirt to move with him. Just for a moment, I saw enough to tell me he was more than half erect, and every bit as impressive as I'd hoped.

I must have leaned on the door handle with some force as I strained forward to get a better look at him, and it rattled, alerting him to the fact he was no longer alone.

If I'd expected him to show concern at being caught abusing office equipment in such an obscene manner, I was disappointed.

'Who's there?' he called out, his voice steady and confident. 'Show yourself.'

Stepping inside, I closed the door behind me, shutting us both into the small dimly lit room with its piles of boxed papers and dry chemical smell.

'Ava,' he said, smirking as he pressed the 'cancel' button, bringing the churning of the photocopier to a welcome halt. 'I might have known it was you.'

'Really, why?' I quirked an eyebrow, awaiting his explanation. Whatever impression Charlie might have gained of me in the months we'd worked alongside each other, I was determined not to let him gain the upper hand in this bizarre encounter.

'Don't think I haven't noticed you're always the first to leave any social event Damon organises – if you bother to turn up for it at all, that is. It's almost like you don't want to be here.'

Had I misjudged him? Was all his slacking to disguise the fact he worked as Damon's eyes and ears on the office floor, covertly observing us between endless games of Angry Birds? Somehow, I couldn't see Charlie being so sneaky; he liked the easy life too much, and his role as the CEO's trusty lap dog had to fulfil that need. He might have had all the advantages over me: youth; ridiculous good looks; a secure position within the company. But, if he thought he'd got me on the back foot with his subtle insinuations, he was wrong.

'Says the man who's sneaked away to photocopy his arse a hundred times. It's not like you're in any position to take the moral high ground, is it?'

'Hey, this was Damon's idea. He wanted to see the look on everyone's face tomorrow morning when they wander in with a hangover to find one of these copies on their desk.' Charlie favoured me with a cold, mocking smile that I itched to wipe from his face. 'He especially wanted to see your reaction.'

'Why, does he think I haven't seen a bare backside before?' I sighed, not at all surprised at how I was viewed by the office hierarchy. 'I've seen things that would make his hair curl. He needs to grow up, Charlie. You both do.'

Charlie laughed, sliding down from the photocopier and bending to pull up his underwear.

'Hey,' I said, my tone causing him to raise his head and look at me in alarm. 'Who said you could do that?'

'I'm sorry? Do I need your permission to get dressed now?'

'Actually, you do. Did you think you were in charge of this situation? That you could treat me like some kind of shrinking virgin?' I shook my head. 'You really don't know me at all, do you? I might not be one of Damon's confidantes, his trusted little social circle, but that doesn't mean I don't have any power around here.'

'Yeah, so what power do you have, exactly?' Charlie's voice had lost a notable amount of its arrogance, and he clutched at the solid body of the photocopier as if for reassurance.

'Oh, the kind of power you can't argue with. The kind that means I can usually get a man to do what I want. Because I see someone like you – someone who wanders round the office in those tight shorts, desperate for all the women to get a good look at everything he's got – and I know that, beneath that cocky exterior, what you want most of all is to be made to show it off.'

'You don't know what you're talking about,' he retorted, but I was certain that, if I could see beneath his shirt, his cock would have risen up, harder than before.

He didn't need to know I'd been taking a stab in the dark when I'd mentioned his desire to be told what to do, but my thrust had hit home, opening up Charlie's submissive core.

'I think I do,' I replied coolly. 'And I'll prove it to you. Step out of your trousers, Charlie.'

He hesitated, obviously wondering whether I was joking. 'Did Damon tell you to do this?'

'Damon? No, he's upstairs, getting off his face on

tequila slammers. He doesn't have a clue I'm down here. No one does. So, are you going to stop asking questions and get out of those trousers, or am I going to have to strip them off you?'

I thought I heard Charlie give a little moan. Forget his adolescent prank with the photocopier; I was the one pushing all the buttons now, and he couldn't fail to respond. Moving as though he was wading through syrup, he bent to unfasten his polished brown brogues, then removed them and his socks before tossing them to one side. He tugged his suit trousers off, hopping from foot to foot, his movements hampered by the underpants still bunched round his ankles.

'Those, too,' I ordered him.

He looked up at me with silent appeal, as though hoping I might change my mind and allow him to pull them up, but I stood firm. Off came the white hipster-cut briefs, the designer's name visible on the waistband as he added it to the pile of clothing I was forcing him to make.

'OK, so you've made your point,' Charlie said. 'Have we finished now?'

'Oh, Charlie, you really aren't learning, are you?' I addressed him with a slow shake of my head. 'We don't finish till you're standing there, bare-arsed naked.'

Uttering those words had an effect on both of us. Watching Charlie perform his slow enforced strip, I felt my pussy suffuse with urgent heat, juice trickling into the crotch of my cream lace thong. As for Charlie, his cock was pushing at the front of his shirt; if not fully erect, then as close as made no difference.

'The shirt, please, Charlie.' I held out a hand, reinforcing my demand.

'And if I refuse?' he asked.

'Oh, then the real fun begins. How would you like to be face down over the photocopier while I spank you with the plastic ruler sitting on that shelf over there?'

He said nothing, but the look in his eyes told me he'd like that very much indeed. Yet still he fought to regain some semblance of control in a situation that had long since slipped out of his grasp.

'What if someone comes past and sees us? Finds me here, naked?' He gave the word an emphasis I was sure was unconscious. It couldn't fail to tell me that, deep down, he was relishing every moment of his unexpected submission. 'I'd like to see you talk your way out of that.'

'It won't be necessary,' I assured him. 'No one will even think of leaving till the booze runs out. And even then their first thought will be to pile into the wine bar on the other side of the dock and keep the party going. But just say someone comes along – well, there's only one thing more exciting than being forced to display your bare hard cock to one fully clothed woman. And that's having to display it to a group of them.'

'Oh, God ...'

Charlie could no longer pretend he wasn't turned on by what was happening to him. Without my needing to ask again, he shucked his tie before unfastening the buttons of his shirt, starting at the top. Even before he'd reached the bottom, his cock poked through the open shirt front, even longer and thicker than I'd pictured it in those moments of idle speculation when he walked round the office in his clinging Lycra.

At last, the shirt slithered from his grip, leaving him naked. The balance of power in the room had changed; I'd felt its subtle shift begin the moment Charlie had bent to remove his footwear. Questions must be rushing through his mind as he stood before me, hands doing their best to cover his crotch. How had he found himself in this position? Where had I found the strength of purpose to face him down? Why had he undressed for me quite so willingly?

We both knew the answer to that one. Whether he'd ever admitted it or not, I was certain that, deep in the recesses of his mind, Charlie harboured fantasies where he was made to strip bare and display himself to an older, dominant woman.

'Very nice,' I said, eyeing the hard contours of his stomach and chest. 'But I want to get a better look. Put your hands on your head, then turn around. Let me see that cute little arse of yours.'

'Please, Ava ...' His protests were half-hearted. It was no use Charlie pretending he didn't want to do this; he was already linking his fingers behind the back of his head, letting me see every last inch of that thick upwardly straining dick, made all the more prominent by the fact he'd trimmed his pubic bush down to almost nothing.

'Should have known you'd go in for a spot of manscaping,' I commented, as he obeyed my instructions to the letter, making a slow pirouette so I could admire the way his firm gluteal muscles flexed. 'You adore showing it all off, don't you, Charlie?'

'Yes, ma'am,' he muttered, facing me once more so I could see the delectable scarlet flush on his cheeks, clear evidence of his embarrassment.

'It's just a pity I'm the only one here to see it.' I made a show of reaching into my bag, fishing out my phone. 'Maybe I should see if any of the girls upstairs would like to come down and join in the show. Who would you like, Charlie? Julie and her gang? You've teased them all for long enough; it's about time they got to see the real thing. Shame Linda from reception isn't here tonight; I've seen the way she drools when you jog past her desk in those dinky little shorts of yours. Or maybe I should just take your clothes, lock the door and leave you here for the cleaners to find in the morning?'

'Oh, no ...'

He had no way of knowing whether I had any intention

of carrying out my threats, and I watched shame, confusion and need battle for supremacy in his expression.

'Lucky for you I'm not in the mood to share. Tonight, the pleasure's going to be all mine. Lie on the floor, Charlie ...'

I reached under my dress, blessing my foresight in wearing hold-up stockings beneath it. It made the removal of my thong all the easier, ensuring Charlie didn't get so much as a flash of my pussy until the moment I settled myself over his face, enveloping him in hot, wet, excited flesh.

Instructions were no longer necessary. Eagerly, Charlie licked all the way from the pucker of my arse to my clit and back, guided by my gasps of pleasure and the steady tightening of my thigh muscles, until he found the spot that pleased me most. I wished the other girls in the office could see me now, riding the office show-off's face like a woman possessed, his limber tongue moving in wicked little circles over my sensitive nub. Tweaking my nipples through my dress, relishing the bursts of sensation that went hurtling down to my pussy, I ground myself against the bridge of Charlie's nose, unable to hold back my pleasure. I'd wanted to make this last, but it was too good, his technique too practised. I saw flashes of light behind my closed eyelids, sharp and rhythmic as the shuttling of the photocopier, as I came.

Vaguely aware I was in danger of smothering Charlie if I stayed in that position for too long, I climbed off him. He looked up at me eagerly, as if hoping I'd return the compliment, but already I was stepping back into my thong.

'What about me?' he asked. 'Don't I get to come?'

I smiled, using my fingers to rearrange my dishevelled hair, cool and in control once more. 'Of course you do, but you have to make it happen. Wank yourself for me, Charlie.'

What else did he expect? I wondered, smiling at his pout of disappointment. Did he really think he'd get to fuck me, after everything? I leaned back against the nearest shelving unit, watching as he scrambled to his feet. Wrapping a fist around his still rock-hard shaft, he stroked it steadily back and forth.

'And your balls,' I said. 'Play with those lovely big balls for me.'

Obedient to the last, he cupped them in his free hand, rolling and squeezing the steadily tightening globes. I love to watch men as they wank; whatever the style and pressure of stroke they favour, they're all alike in their unswerving dedication to make themselves come, and he was no exception.

Charlie's excitement was the clear equal of mine, and almost before he was ready, it seemed, he was grunting in incoherent bursts and shuddering as the thick come pumped out over his fist.

'Gorgeous,' I purred. 'But don't forget to lick up every

last drop. Or I really will leave you here with nothing to cover your modesty but your tie. Just imagine trying to get all the way back home without your clothes ...'

Without a murmur, Charlie began the task of licking his fingers clean of spunk. The expression in his eyes as he did told me his mind had seized on the idea of being made to streak through the office, causing his cock to stiffen once more.

Deciding he'd suffered enough for one night – and clearly enjoyed every moment of it – I opened the door, causing him a moment's panic as he hunted round for his discarded underwear. Not that he needed to worry; this floor was silent, the rest of the staff still partying upstairs.

'Time to say goodnight, Charlie. But we'll talk again tomorrow. I have some thoughts about the impending office reorganisation I'd like to share with you, and I'm sure you'll be very interested in what I have to propose ...'

There was no way he'd let Damon make me redundant now. Charlie needed the special brand of humiliation only I could offer him; needed to find himself in a situation where nudity was enforced on him whenever and wherever I decided. And my discreet corner office would be the perfect place. No more slacking for him; not when I could have him naked under my desk, down on his knees and ready to give my pussy whatever attention it required.

For the first time in longer than I could remember, I looked forward to going into work the following day.

Interview With The Vamp
Scarlett Rush

'Kiss my arse,' she said.

'Sorry?' I almost fainted at her words.

It was not your average response to a question during a job interview but she was not your average woman. She was Portia DeLacy. She was feted throughout the City, perhaps as much for her looks as for her talents. Before her father moved up to boardroom level, he had been a legendary trader and had taught her all he knew. If anything she knew more, and she was still only 33. She was the one we wanted above all. We had moved heaven and earth to create the opportunity to get her on board, and to ensure we could get her on the cheap. We could have just paid her the going rate but we either couldn't or didn't want to afford her. Anyway, like a good many investment bankers, doing things by the book wasn't really our way.

I was glad I had met her once before, if only to get past the first throes of my inferiority complex, the part which would have me staring dumbly at her just like I did in Margaux's wine bar when we made our initial approach. I don't usually do fish impressions but I did one that night, wordlessly opening and closing my mouth as I tried to think of anything to say that wouldn't mark me out as a jumped-up HR nobody, elevated to seniority through good looks rather than by merit. She gave me little notice that night, regarding me as I did my best haddock impression, impassively holding my gaze before evaluating the rest of me with a cursory up and down examination. She was in a different league to me and she knew it, so she hadn't troubled herself with paying me any further attention.

She gave no indication that she even recognised me as she came into the interview room. She had already sat herself in the padded leather chair before I had a chance to offer my outstretched hand. I was positioned some three feet opposite her, not behind a desk. We wanted no barriers here. I was selected because they felt I would have the greatest affinity with her. It was a huge opportunity for me so I didn't persuade them otherwise, although I am five years her junior and have nothing like her poise and steel. I've got my share of good looks, I guess, but I'm blonde and blue-eyed and feel ditzy and irrelevant alongside someone with her dark sophistication. Her long hair was as jet black as her clothes and painted nails. Her skin was pale and flawless and nearly devoid of make-up. On that night at Margaux's, she had worn a cut of blusher and a darker, claret shade of lipstick as opposed to the crimson colouring of today. Her eyeliner had been heavier then too, and above each eyebrow was stuck a neat line of tiny discs in metallic purple, matching her single small nose stud. It all gave her a posh-goth look that had seemed so sexy yet impenetrable. It had made me tremble. She was like some goddess of the undead who just happened to know all there was to know about mergers and acquisitions. Her reputation aside, before I met her I knew little about her other than she sounded like she had been named after a German sports car. After a mere ten minutes in her company, I knew that she was everything I would wish to be. After coming back from Margaux's, I'd had to finger myself twice before my boyfriend got home, and even that didn't cure me of her.

However, she was over the barrel now as far as we were concerned. This didn't seem to bother her and she batted away my first couple of questions as if it were her and not me conducting the interview. Her poise and indifference unnerved me. I was glad of the chance to be the one to secure her services but unprepared for her bullish demeanour. We needed her more than we could ever admit and I was the one who had to make sure it happened. This was a daunting task considering our status as mid-table players and the current financial knocks we had recently endured. She was to be our saviour. Get her on board and everyone would take us seriously. She might only stay a year but she would yield us the benefits of ten traders combined. It had been suggested that, should I succeed in getting her, a tidy bonus would be coming my way. Somehow, though, and when I looked back I realised that it had never actually been stated, it was also hinted that if I failed I would most likely be joining her in the hunt for a new employer. That's how desperately they wanted her.

I had never felt out of my depth in an interview situation until now. I silently cursed the board's decision to have the proceedings conducted on a one-to-one basis rather than with a panel, more of a cosy chat than an interview. Every time I tried to get back to my agenda she rode roughshod over me. She sapped any power and initiative I thought I might have. She leaned towards me in her chair, her hands gripping the front edge, as if she was ready at any moment to spring up and go, to dismiss my offers with derision and leave me dead in the water. She was chewing me up and spitting me out, and I simply couldn't shift the visions of her that had accompanied all my frantic wanking sessions. I should have been in total control but I was lost.

To soften the blow of a low salary offer, I had been given various other juicy inducements to tempt her, although her main incentive was that she would very soon be out of a job. This was by no means common knowledge but *we* of course knew it, which is why we had made our approach in the first place. Her current employers, Maccaby Fitch, had given her the choice of jumping before she was pushed, having been made aware of some of her dodgier dealings. Once upon a time, a blind eye would have been turned to her nefarious ways, but in the current climate of mistrust they could not be countenanced.

We knew she was to be forced out even before she did. We have a mole inside Maccaby, paid a retainer to leak certain information to us while still receiving a hefty salary from his legitimate employers. Never underestimate the greed of bankers! In fact, it was this very mole who leaked her business indiscretions to the Maccaby board in the first place, thus allowing us to engineer the poaching of one of their most valued assets. It was all clever stuff, if exceedingly underhand.

Her reputation would suffer terribly if the truth became public, and any future employer would be tarnished by association if they were stupid enough to take her on. She would need to secure a new position before anyone got wind of the scandal. If we could sneak in with a job offer – a half-decent one but nothing like what she would currently be on – she might feel she had no option but to accept. The longer she waited, the more chance there was of her secret emerging, and thus ruining her. Our inside knowledge meant that we held all the aces. I was even authorised, as a last resort only, to make her aware we knew about her current position. The inference was that, if *we* knew, then everyone else was going to know very quickly, unless she put her name to our contract. I already knew this tactic was doomed to failure. She was way too proud to give in to blackmail. She would have taken her chances rather than bow to us, and she would have torn me to pieces for my impudence before she left here. No, that was one ploy that would definitely blow up in my face.

I needed to use more guile to ensnare her, but she wasn't even listening to my offers, demanding instead to be told of the company's current strategies and successes, none of which I knew much about.

'This is ridiculous!' she suddenly exclaimed.

I was trying to recall my last words to see what had provoked the outburst, but I was keenly aware that she had found me out. She knew she was talking to the monkey and not to the organ grinder. I felt like a waiter or a servant rather than the one presenting her with the very opportunity she must have been crying out for.

'Sorry, what is ridiculous?' I managed to stammer.

'It's so fucking hot in here – I can't even concentrate. I shall have to take my tights off.'

I don't know what I planned to say but it came out

more as a blubbing sob, rather than any coherent words. Had she said *tights*? I didn't even have time to ponder this further before she was up and out of her seat. I thought she was going to lean over and hit me. Instead, she was reaching down for the hem of her pencil skirt and slowly pulling it up, working it inch by inch over the firm thighs showing white through the gaps in her fishnets. It must have been some surreal, wonderful dream, one that I would wake from at any second. Until I did, my eyes just kept following the slow rise of her skirt as it was eased past her wide hips and bunched around her middle. I was vaguely aware that my fish impression had returned and that the wetness behind my bottom lip was close to dribbling out, but I was way more conscious of the fact that she had no knickers on under her tights.

There was a pause, perhaps for effect or perhaps in a moment for her of rare reticence, and then her tights were indeed coming down, slowly revealing her porcelain beauty. I could hear the static prickle of the nylon sliding over her smoothness, and imagined the little goose-bump shiver it would induce across her shaven skin. Off came the tights, gathering momentum as her legs tapered. Soon she was sitting again, her high heels kicked off so that she could raise each foot in turn to peel the hosiery from her toes. It didn't quite seem to be done as a striptease, more out of the necessity that she had claimed. Her shoes were replaced and she rested back fully composed, as if awaiting my next question, even though she hadn't actually pulled her skirt back down. Totally unperturbed, she sat with her legs slightly parted and the neat dark split of her pussy clearly visible. There was nothing I could do but stare.

'What's wrong?' she said, with some annoyance. 'Have you never seen a bare cunt before?'

The vulgar word sent a jolt through my sex and made me gasp out loud. In my dreams I hadn't pictured her mound as completely hairless, but now I could see how perfect it looked so utterly exposed. There were no traces of stubble or blemishes on her little bump. It had the same airbrushed quality of the quims I snuck secret looks at in my boyfriend's dirty magazines. Her thin inner labia were very pale pink, almost the same colour as the skin on her thighs. They were barely protruding delicate petals, so unlike my own plump lips that looked engorged and lewd when I was aroused. But she gave no indication that she was turned on at all, that this brazen exposure was any more than what she had said: a requirement to cool down so that she could regain her focus.

'You are still staring at my cunt,' she said, making me jump.

I mumbled some kind of apology and hastily cast my eyes down at my notes, feeling ridiculous that this bare-fannied beauty could still somehow make me appear to be the unprofessional one. I was aware that my face had turned bright red. My eyes picked out some random question but behind them was the vision of her lovely pussy. I had no idea what she was saying in response. I only knew that her puss must taste and smell sublime, that its softness would be unique. They can be so vulgar, can pussies, so fat and open and crying out to be filled. Mine was. My boyfriend often called it my 'snatch' in the heat of the moment, just to enforce my vision of it as a greedy, distended gash demanding attention. Hers though, hers was pristine and truly irresistible.

'You are staring again,' she chided. 'What is it about it that you find so fascinating? Is it because it is hairless? You *do* shave your cunt, don't you? I couldn't take a job from someone who didn't even have the decency to shave in the morning. Show it to me.'

'*What?*'

Had she just asked me to show her my cunt?

'Take your knickers off and show me. Assuming you took the trouble to put any underwear on today.'

My head was a total mess. She, who actually *hadn't* troubled to wear knickers, was sitting there with her quim on display and asking me to show me my own, yet somehow I was the one being made to sound like a slut. Stranger still, my primary reluctance to do as she said was less through the keen embarrassment I should have been feeling, and more from the fact that she had said she wouldn't take a job offered by someone with a hairy minge! I clipped mine close and kept it tidy for sure, but I always left it with some covering. She wouldn't like that!

'I can't,' I said, trying and failing to put on a mask of indifference.

'Then I shall have to leave,' she replied.

This was beyond ridiculous. I felt a surge of panic at her threat to go but still, incredibly, I had equal jitters at having to do as she asked and somehow offend her by displaying my pubic hair. There was no way that this was the true reason she wanted me bare, but at the same time there was no hint whatsoever that she saw this as a remotely sexual scenario. I glanced over towards the door, seeking any excuse, but this inter-view was one of *the* most private business dealings this company would ever have and we both knew there was no chance of any interruption. I could strip naked and turn cartwheels and no one but she would ever know. I was drying up and quivering but she made to leave and that spurred me into action. As swiftly as possible I stood, slipped off my knickers and sat down again with my skirt pulled up to expose my lower half. I kept my thighs firmly together but the quickest of glances downwards confirmed that a small strip of pubic hair was indeed visible at my crotch. I cleared my throat and tried to appear business-like as she nonchalantly examined me.

'Open your legs,' she said.

I paused briefly, then hauled in my breath and complied, again trying to appear calm.

'Which hand do you masturbate with?' she asked.

I began to protest but she merely raised one eyebrow as a reminder that she would leave if I didn't behave immediately.

'My right one,' I said, trying to pretend to myself that she had asked which one I shook hands with, or which one I was going to slap myself hard around the face with as soon as I had got her name on the contract and got her out of here. Was my job worth this humiliation? Yes, was the answer, and worse still was my underlying reluctance to have her cover herself up again.

'Put your right hand down between your legs and open yourself up with two fingers, so I can see inside you.'

I was not just quivering but also shaking now, seeing her gaze locked on my snatch, knowing what I had to do for this mouth-watering woman. I was struggling to find my breath, my thoughts already flying forward to what I thought might happen in the next blissful minutes. I had only ever wilfully shown my fanny to one other girl and she had wanted to stick her fingers up it and fuck me. Surely this scenario could be no different? I parted my thighs as far as they would go, reached down and spread my lips apart with two fingers, pushing forward to give her a better view inside me. She looked but her expression did not change.

78

'Just as I thought,' she said. 'Your cunt is wet, you dirty bitch. Keep it held apart to help dry it out while you ask your next question.'

My head spun. She didn't want to fuck me after all, she just wanted me to air my snatch and go on asking dumb questions that she wasn't even answering. She was a mad woman and I had to secure her services or lose my own job. Almost asphyxiating, I held my notes in my left hand and scoured the pages for any kind of question, still holding myself wide open for her unfaltering gaze.

'What percentage of your client base do you think you can bring over to us?' I asked, thinking each next word to be the stupidest I had ever said in my life.

'Kiss my arse,' she said.

'Sorry?' I almost fainted at her words.

She shifted forward to the edge of her seat, leaned back and raised her knees, clasping behind them to keep her legs up. I could see the creamy-white softness of her bum cheeks squashed to the seat, and now nestled between them her anus. It was as delectable as her puss; a tight gathering of flesh, again barely darker than the surrounding skin, with a little oval hole at its centre.

'You want me to take this job, don't you?' she said, softly this time.

I nodded mutely, my eyes needing to close now that I was squeezing my throbbing clit, but desperate also to stay open and feast on her rudeness.

'Then get over here and kiss my arse.'

It was blackmail but I didn't care. I had never wanted to do anything more in my life. I shuffled off my chair and knelt between her legs. She was even more perfect up close. She looked smooth and vulnerable. The thought of a stubbly chin gorging on this delicacy was unthinkable. She smelled fresh and fragrant. I gradually came forward, closing my eyes as I felt the contact of her little bum-hole against my pursed wet lips. I gave her the tenderest kiss I have given anyone, pressing gently and applying just a little suction, forcing her to sigh.

'French kiss it,' she breathed. 'Use the tip of your tongue all around it and then push it up inside me.'

It didn't even seem dirty, just sublime. I teased the slightly firmer flesh of her little ring and felt elated that it made her tremble. Then I sucked harder upon it and pushed on, trying to force her open and taste inside her. She let go her grip on her knees, holding my hair instead with one hand to stop me from becoming too greedy. Her other hand came down between my nose and her sex, one finger slipping up inside her, the labia closing guardedly around it so that I still could not see her wetness. Her breathing became more erratic as she pressed the finger in deep and stirred it around. I wanted her to climax with me kissing her bottom but the glistening digit slipped back out of her and she pushed me gently away.

'Sit back on your chair and open your legs,' she said.

I spread myself open for her once more, this time proud of the fatness of my cunt and the flowing juices that coated it. She bent to collect her tights from the floor and my heart jolted. But she was moving her chair forward, shifting closer so that our knees were nearly touching, and she was handing me the clump of netted material.

'You are still too wet. Push this in there to soak it all up.'

She had singled out one leg of the tights now resting in my palm, offering it to me. I couldn't speak now. I took the material between my fingers, feeling the light coarseness of it, trying to feel any essence of her that had been transferred into it. I gently pushed it against my hot hole and felt the tiny electric rasp. Toe first I slowly pushed the leg of the tights inside me, just as she had instructed. It was a strange feeling, slightly discomforting, mostly glorious, not just because it was filling me but because they were *hers*. I kept pressing until I was stuffed and the crotch of the tights was half inside me. This was the best part, knowing that her delicious bare quim had touched and dampened that very material, like her perfect cunt was now touching mine.

'Rub your clit now.'

I didn't see her say it because my eyes were closed. I have never played with myself in front of anyone before but I did her bidding instantly, not because of the stupid fucking job, but because I was desperate to. I pinched and pulled and frigged myself and imagined her bottom all over my face, and of my tongue right up inside her. I could feel myself drenching the fabric. I felt a slight tug on the material inside me and opened my eyes to see that she too had her legs splayed apart and she had taken the other leg of the tights and was feeding it into her little pussy. As she pushed more fabric inside herself, the part inside of me was pulled out bit by bit, giving that same tantalising rasp against my sensitive interior. It was harsh but exquisite, just as she was. As each scrap of the coarse stocking was pulled clear, the thrilling tingle it sent through me was magnified by the sight of her fingers forcing the other leg into her tight slit. As soon as the toe end slipped from my cunt I plunged my fingers in there instead and came all over them, watching her rub her clit as urgently as I had just done.

She came with a tremor that jiggled her chair, biting her bottom lip and screwing her eyes closed as she wound the material around her hand and slowly eased it back out of her pussy. Her climax hit her as hard as mine had but we both knew it wasn't enough. Still breathing hard, still shivering, she took me by the hair and pulled me down so that we were kneeling and kissing on the floor. Her mouth was as hot and silken as I had dreamed her pussy to be. I wanted to go on kissing her but she was forcing me down to the floor and scrambling around so that we were both on our sides, facing each other though top to tail, and she was wrapping her thighs around my head. And then suddenly it was her pussy pressed to my mouth and I was tonguing her and slurping her nectar down. I knew I would never taste anything more glorious or experience anyone as beautiful as her again. I couldn't wait to see her every day at work and out of it too, if she would only let me. I would do anything and everything she asked, serve her if she so wished, kiss her bum and eat her juicy cunt whenever she told me to. I would pray that once again she would eat me as hungrily as now. I would gleefully give up my boyfriend today to become her possession. I would even share her if I had to.

Her slippery puss was spread across my lips and I tasted her depths, squashed hard into her, my nose breathing her sweet anus. She was taking me nearer every second and I sucked hard upon her clit, just as she was doing to me. I felt her nails dig into my bum and the crush of her thigh at the side of my head. We came together, writhing again and suppressing our screams, the juices flowing out on to our faces. We were quiet as we untangled ourselves and got our shaking legs to propel us back to our seats. It was the most incredible experience of my life. All I could do was grin at her.

Eventually, with my heart still banging with the excitement of it all, I said, 'So, can I inform my bosses that you will be joining us very soon?'

'Yes,' she said, smiling, 'you can. In fact, sweetie, you

83

can tell them anything you like if it makes you feel happy, but I won't be signing your contract any time ever. Do you think I want to work for a tin-pot firm that can't even afford decent air conditioning? I only did this interview because I wanted to fuck you. I guessed by your mouth that you would have a fat, succulent cunt and my instincts are seldom wrong. If you had stuck around that night at Margaux's, I could have had you then and saved you a morning's work. Plus, if you *had* stayed, that guy from Bierbaum wouldn't have had the chance to get to me. He spotted you that night and smelled a rat. As soon as you left, he softened me up with champagne and somehow got me to reveal my intention to seek new employers. He offered me a job on the spot, for three times what you are willing to pay. I start with them next month, once I get back from my holiday.'

She removed her shoes and put her tights back on, careful not to ruin them with her black painted toenails. She didn't seem to mind the dampness against her skin or the fact that the material was now scented with our rudeness.

'Bierbaum's is a proper firm,' she said. 'Maybe if you find yourself looking for work in the near future I can put in a good word for you.'

She gave me a big smile, picked up my sodden knickers, stood up and calmly tossed them on to my lap, then turned on her high heels and walked right out of the room.

The Going Down Chronicles
Chrissie Bentley

The Princess Hyacinth Books readers club never really caught on that strongly. Every month, the same dozen or so girls – women, or whatever we call ourselves these days – would gather on the main floor of the store after closing, arrange ourselves in a vague circle of hard plastic chairs, and try to find some interesting points to make about whichever tome we'd most recently been assigned. But, invariably, half the group had not finished it, a few had not even started it, and the one lass who did get from cover to cover only did so because she was new to the group, and thought that's what she was meant to do.

Wrong. The book club wasn't about books. It was about getting away from the house for an hour or so, to sit and talk with a group of ladies who were fast becoming very good friends – Janet, a fifty-something housewife with weary eyes and flyaway hair; Lesley, a college graduate with a vicious sense of humor and a job in computers; Sandra, the no-nonsense grandmother who barely said a word at her first three visits, but then opened up into one of the loveliest people you've ever met, and so on. Every fourth Wednesday, we'd troop into the store at a little after six, take our seats and take out our books – and promptly start talking about something else.

This week was different, though. Patsy, the once-gorgeous, now merely glamorous woman who'd owned the store for the past quarter-century, and who launched the book club in the first place, had decided (to herself) to shake things up a little and order up a book that she said might give us something else to talk about, other than our usual chorus of cackles and gossip. If you want to find your own copy, it's called *The Body Project* ... I can't remember the author's name (this all happened a couple of years ago), but it's basically a long and somewhat rambling study of how society's perceptions of young women have changed over the past hundred years.

I'm looking at the notes I made as I read it (I'll confess, I'm a compulsive note-taker), few of which really recommend the book back to me today. But then I come to a paragraph that simply leaps off the page, bold red ink, every letter two lines high. FIRST BLOWJOB – COERCION, NOT CONSENT. WHAT CRAP THIS WOMAN WRITES.

What exactly did she write? I can't remember. But it

was very different from anything I experienced the first time I took a man inside my mouth, and, from conversations I'd had with my girlfriends over the years, it was very different for them as well. Now I was wondering – well, we'd talked about almost everything else at the book club, why not oral sex?

The meeting was already underway when I arrived at the store, and I was astonished to discover that, for perhaps the first time in all the years I'd been attending the club, everybody had something to say about the book; opinions that ranged from outright admiration to sheer hatred. Sandra, especially, had an arsenal of opinions – she was old enough to have lived through the events covered in the early chapters of the book; could remember what it was like to be a gangly teenager in a Midwest steel town at the height of the depression; to be married at eighteen to a man twice her age ... Tonight, her snorts of derision were probably audible all the way back there as well.

I sat quietly, while the others finished up the line of thought they were already pursuing, and then made my play. The book was too negative, too whiney and far too generalized. 'But I think the line that got me was about halfway down page –' whatever page it was.

There was a rustling as the others found the page, a silence as they read down, and then an arched eyebrow from Laura, a prim little thing who bred poodles – for a living or a hobby, I never found out. 'What's wrong with that?'

'I just thought, again, it was too negative, too generalized. One quote from one bad experience.'

'Probably because ten quotes from ten bad experiences would have been overstating the obvious.'

Patsy stepped in. 'Is that you speaking, or have you actually asked around?'

Laura's voice took on a defensive edge. 'Well, let's ask around, then. Anybody want to start the ball rolling? Tell us all about the first time you sucked a guy's cock?'

There was a moment's hesitation; then another. For a moment, the room was silent. Then Sandra spoke up. 'Why not? But maybe we should move into one of the back rooms, call our folks to say we'll be home late. And someone should run out to the liquor store and get in some wine.'

The others looked around; a silent nod of consent passed around the room, and there was a cacophony of bleeps and clicks as a dozen cell phones hummed into action. I was astonished – nobody backed out, nobody remembered an urgent appointment and, as they hung up from their calls, nobody had been apprised of an unforeseen family emergency that demanded they rush home immediately. Patsy was already moving the chairs into the backroom suite that was normally her office; I was collecting cash from the others, to fund the liquor run. A bottle each would probably do it ...

As I walked, I recalled my own first time. His name was Marty, we were at college, fooling around late one night. We'd been sleeping together for a while now, but, though I'd often thought about it, I'd never actually done it. Lying there now, my eyes were fixed on his cock, bigger now than I'd ever believed it could be, and alive with a danger I wasn't sure I could face. What if he came in my mouth – would I be able to take it? Would I choke, would I bite him? Would I throw up? I wondered if I'd have any warning beforehand, if he'd say something, or maybe I'd know from his movements. I eyed the liquid that was already oozing out of the slit in the tip of his helmet. OK, just a little bit.

I leaned forward and let my tongue dart out to touch him; pulled it back, conscious of the long thin string of viscous liquid that now joined my mouth to his cock. But I couldn't taste anything, so I leaned forward again and ran my tongue through the thickening pool, my mind so set on the quest at hand that, as Marty let out a moan of sheer pleasure, I scarcely even heard him; barely connected it with anything I had done.

The liquid danced lightly on my tongue, a delicate tang that teased, rather than tasted, and I needed more. This time my tongue swirled across the end of his cock, across the crest and then down and around, to pick off any drops of dew that might be hiding beneath the thick ridge of the head. My lips brushed his flesh – stop writhing behind me, I'm busy – and I closed them over the thick end and sucked slightly, drawing that mystery juice from the depths, then taking him a little bit deeper, just a little bit more, feeling cheated as the full taste of his juices continued to elude me.

My mouth widened, stretching to accommodate the full bulk of his cock head; I felt my teeth scrape against his flesh and hoped that gasp from behind me was not one of pain. Then, just as I was convinced that I could not open my mouth any wider, there was a sudden magical moment of release as the head of his cock slipped full into my mouth, and my lips closed over his steel-stiff shaft. 'Gotcha,' I thought, and my sucking grew greedier, hungrier.

I felt his hips begin to move rhythmically below me. Two can play at that game. Deliberately timing my movements to oppose his, I started moving back, using my mouth as a warm, tight pussy – only it was a pussy whose every movement I could control. Tight, then loose; gentle, then hard. I let my teeth sink into his skin in a brief nip, then pushed my tongue to the same spot as a kind of cushion. Now I could taste him, hot, sweet, salty ... but it was different to before, stronger, deeper; I wondered how many other secret flavors this man was holding back from me.

I withdrew him from my mouth; there was a satisfying 'plop' as my lips released him, and another deep groan; then I wrapped my lips again across the head, concentrating all my energies, all my taste buds, on that one sensitive area, sucking, swirling, swamping him in saliva. I breathed warm air on his skin and he twitched; I held him lightly between two fingers, and smeared the end of his cock across my face, enjoying the sensation of hot moistness as it traced livid, liquid lines across my lips, cheeks and chin.

His moans and gasps were almost non-stop now, an animal backdrop to my own adventuring; I was glad he seemed to be enjoying himself, and I was shocked to realize his fingers were inside me, punching deep inside my own soaked sex, the rhythmic squelching setting up a secondary symphony behind his gasps.

After pausing for a moment, I plunged him back into my mouth, timing my own movements to match his fingers, slowing when he slowed, faster as he quickened the pace. I could feel my cunt pulse around his driving digits as his cock moved effortlessly in and out of my mouth, and I lost myself to the exquisite motion, drinking in his hot hard flesh and feeling for the first time the hairs on his balls brush the tip of my nose, a dainty tickle that fascinated me. I pushed my chin forward, wondering if I could reach the other hairs above his cock, and a rough scratching sensation informed me that I could. I paused, nestled my nose in the folds of his balls, resting the tip of my chin on his stomach, then I closed my teeth gently round the base of his cock, as though marking out my territory – this is mine!

Marty's fingers were still slamming me; I wondered how many he had inside me now, I felt like I was stretching further than I ever had before, but the slickness of my juices dulled any sensation beyond the most exquisite sense of pressure. I picked up my pace again, sliding up and down that long greasy pole; then, feeling my jaw tire, I slowed and concentrated back at the head, in – out; in – out; in … oh! There was no warning, or, if there was, I never heard it; no telltale pulsing, or perhaps I never felt it. But there was no mistaking the hot, hot jet that sprayed into my mouth; that shot across my face as I jerked, startled, away; that blasted from the cock I held just inches away from my face.

For a moment, I almost let it go; for a second, I felt panic stir in my stomach. But then my mind took over again, calm and analytical, questioning and curious. Gulping down the come that was already sliding towards the back of my throat, I closed my mouth firmly over his still dribbling cock, and guided more of his flavor on to my tongue, sucking until there was none left to savor, while his hardness slowly ebbed away on my lips.

Coercion? I'd like to have seen someone try to stop me!

Sandra had already started her tale by the time I got

back to the store, although Patsy whispered that I'd only missed some background – who her husband was, how she met him, that sort of thing. Now she was preparing for her wedding night, with her nose buried in a copy of *Ideal Marriage*, a scholarly how-to guide that was *the* bible of 'how to do it' for most of the 20th century.

'It was going fine. And then I got to the section on genital kisses. I remember I had to read that paragraph three times before I was sure I'd not imagined it – that all the other things I'd read hadn't twisted my mind so much that I was reading "genital" everywhere. I don't think I was horrified, though. My feelings about sex – you have to remember, I was only eighteen – were completely ambivalent; I thought of it like going to the dentist, I might not like it, I might not know what was going to happen, but it had to be done and that was all there was to it. So I might as well get on with it.

'The idea of kissing his genitals, though, wouldn't leave my mind, even when I was reading about other things. So I made up my mind. I didn't know how things were going to happen that night, or what he was expecting to happen. But I decided I'd just do it like it said in the book, whether he asked me to or not. Then, when it was over, we'd go on to the next thing.'

'You really didn't have a clue, did you?' Patsy smiled.

Sandra shook her head. 'Not a clue. The most we'd ever done before we married was kiss lips. He may have squeezed my breast once, but I think it was an accident. So no, as far as I was concerned, there was a routine you had to follow – that's what *Ideal Marriage* seemed to be saying, and I was going to follow it.

'We went to bed and he was holding on to me immediately, pressing himself against me. I could feel his – I thought of it as his *thing* – pushing into my thigh, not as hot as I thought it would be, but very hard, and he was trying to direct my hand down toward with it, casually, as though he thought I wouldn't notice. So I touched it, and he groaned so loud I thought I'd hurt him – I let go and leapt back, and it took him a while to reassure me that everything was OK. I put my hand back there, and he had his hand on me. Anyway, I don't need to tell you all that stuff, but finally he was trying to roll on top of me and I was trying to remember what it said in the book, that this was the climax of our lovemaking, and that the genital kiss should come first, so I pushed him back, and then just dived down there, held his thing as straight as I could, and kissed it.

'He swore. I'd never heard him so much as cuss before, but he almost cried out a loud goddamit. I was sure the other people in the hotel must have heard him too, but then he said, "Do that again," so I did, and I kept on doing it, my lips pursed tightly together, hard pecks smack on the tip. A genital kiss. "Not so hard," he said, so I started doing it more lightly. "Not so fast." So I slowed down, and I was wondering whether I'd ever get it right, because now he wasn't making a sound. Poor man, later I realized he was wondering how to say what he actually wanted me to be doing, but of course I didn't know that, so I just kept on kissing him there, until finally he reached down and held my head still with one hand, and started pushing his thing against my mouth with the other.

'I didn't know *what* he was doing! My lips were tight together, and I could feel him pushing them back against my teeth, but I was so worried that I might bite him there that I didn't dare open my mouth, until the pressure was so hard that finally I had to – and there he was, inside my mouth. Not far, probably not even half an inch, and my jaw was straining around him, but now I could feel him moving his hips, and trying to rock my head up and down, and ... I don't know, it was like a light suddenly went on in my head, because this wasn't anything like I'd read in the book, but it seemed to be what he wanted, so I took a deep breath through my nose, and let him push himself in. And that was it, because suddenly he pulled out again, let out another cuss, and his stuff just came spurting out all over his hand.

'So it wasn't pleasant, it wasn't unpleasant. It was just something I did that he enjoyed. It was different later – you get to know someone, you get to know what they like, and soon I was doing it and knowing exactly what I was doing. But that was my first time – so who's next?'

Laura. Somehow I knew it would be Laura. And I knew it would be unpleasant – the brutish boyfriend who couldn't believe that she wouldn't put out, but he was willing to put up with it if she'd just do this one thing for him. So she did it, and she hated it, and just to make things worse, he didn't pull out when he came, he simply shot his load in her mouth, and then held her head down so that she didn't have any choice but to swallow it. And, of course, he dumped her the next week anyway, and the whole bitter brief experience probably ruined the sex life of every guy she's ever dated since then.

'My first was almost like that.' Patsy. 'We were making out in his car, and suddenly his pants were open and it was in my hand, so ... I knew what to do, I was jerking him, and wishing I'd rolled my sleeve up first, because it was a new blouse and I didn't want to get his ick all over it. Then he started pushing my head down – not hard, but insistently, and part of me was thinking, "Oh God, he wants me to do *that*," and the other part was, "Well, maybe it won't be so gross," so I let him.

'But then I got cold feet and thought, "Well, I don't want it in my mouth," so I did it like Sandra, I just started kissing him, and then I thought I'd lick him for a change, and, Christ, I thought I was going to come there and then, because it suddenly flashed into my mind what I was doing, a really vivid mental picture of my tongue running up this huge – well, I thought it was huge – shaft, and I could see the colors of his helmet, and there was that wonderful smell, and I just wanted to coil my tongue around and around. I still didn't want him inside my mouth, but I wanted my mouth all around him, licking his cock and his balls, and he was going wild, gasping and swearing, and saying my name over and over, and how much he loved me, and no one had ever done it like this before … which probably wasn't quite the right thing to say, because I didn't want to think that anyone had ever done this to him before.

'Which is when I had this really weird thought, wondering if I could give him a hickey on it. So I tilted my head, and got him between my teeth, about halfway down, and I started to suck as hard as I could, until I could taste the blood coming to the surface. I was rubbing his balls with my free hand, and when he came, it was so funny because, where I'd been worrying about my new blouse, I'd completely forgotten my hair, which I'd only had done that afternoon. I don't know if you've ever tried to get great globs of dried come out of your hair, but it's not easy. Even in the shower, it just got stickier, I ended up having to cut it out with nail scissors. But I'll tell you one thing. That hickey was still there a week later!'

My story was next, in all its greedy, greasy detail and, as I looked around the group to see who would go next, I really wasn't sure if that was shock or envy that I saw flash back from at least four pairs of eyes. But, when

Madeleine cleared her throat, I knew that anything I'd had to say on the subject was about to be placed firmly in the shade.

You only had to look at Madeleine to know that she was a man-eater, in every sense of the word. She had one of those mouths that were simply made to swallow cock, and the kind of body that made every cock want to be swallowed. Just walking down the road with her, as I sometimes did after book club, every guy on the street would turn to look at her, while she kept up a running commentary, just loud enough for me to hear, on why she would, or wouldn't, go home with each of them.

'I used to practice on bananas.' She paused. 'Really, before I ever had a guy, I used to practice on bananas. I'd peel 'em back and see how far down my throat I could stick one. The first wet dream I ever had, I was blowing the guy next door, and, when I did start dating, I almost went mad waiting for him to make the first move, just so I could get him in my mouth.

'None of the other stuff interested me. I didn't care about losing my virginity, or having my tits felt, or my pussy licked. I just wanted to suck a cock and it was ridiculous, because you'd think every guy in the world would have been queuing up at my door, but I went through four boyfriends before I even got my hands down somebody's trousers. And, when it did finally look like happening, the idiot got so excited so quickly that he'd come all over my hand before I'd even got his pants down.

'Anyway, one night I was babysitting for a family down the road. They just wanted me to stay until their older kids got home. They'd gone to a party or something. There was a boy who was about a year older than me, and his sister who was a couple of years younger. And the boy offered to walk me home. He didn't know I only lived about five doors away, so I took him in the opposite direction entirely, and we wound up on the soccer fields. It was pitch black, and we just started fooling around. Not kissing or anything, more like wrestling. He'd grabbed my wrap and started running off with it, and I caught him, and we were on the ground, he was sitting on my chest, pinning me down, and I was trying to get him off me, by tickling his ribs.

'He was squirming, and pushing forward, his crotch was right in my face, and that was when I noticed that he was H-A-R-D, hard. Now, I should mention that it was early summer, and really warm, so all he had on down there was a pair of shorts, so this was a real tent-pole sticking out, and I thought, "Well, it's halfway there anyway," so I just opened my mouth and in he went.

'It was nothing like I'd expected. A lot bigger, for a start. Fatter. I'd never found a banana that thick, so that surprised me. And it tasted different as well, I'd never really thought about what a cock would taste like, I just assumed that it would be a lot like any other part of the body, your arm or something, so that surprised me as well, although not as much as I surprised him. I think it took him a moment or two to realize precisely what was happening, but suddenly he was "What are you doing?"

'Now, you all know that it's impossible to speak with something that big in your mouth, so I just made a muffled mmpphh-mmpphhh sort of sound, and held on a little tighter in case he tried to pull away – which he did, because I think he was getting a little scared now, in case I bit it off maybe, or didn't know what I was doing and might freak out when I found out.

'So I let go and said, "What do you think I'm doing? If you're going to go round sticking things like that in people's faces, what do you expect to happen?" That completely threw him, so, while he was thinking about it, I just reached in and popped his tackle out of one of his shorts legs, then put it back in my mouth.

'The problem was, he was so big that I couldn't do anything once it was in there, I couldn't suck, I could barely move my tongue, I just lay there with him sticking in there. So I took hold of his hips and started swaying him back and forth, until I could feel him sliding in and out. And, of course, he figured that out very quickly. He leaned forward, with his hands on the ground, and started fucking my mouth.

'He was so gentle about it and, as my muscles began to relax, I found I could do all sorts of little tricks, little sucks and nips, and he was moving faster and faster, and it was so smooth, my eyes were closed and this really was the best thing I'd ever felt in my entire life, the happiest I'd ever been, just lying there with him moving in and out of me. My lips were tracing the little bumps and veins on his prick, and the ridge, and the smooth curve, it was everything I'd ever dreamed it could be and more.

'I didn't ever want it to end, even when my mouth started aching, but of course it had to. He was thrusting harder and harder, until suddenly he jerked himself out and, in the same instant, I felt his come whip across my cheeks and my lips, which was great because that's the one thing I'd never actually figured out how to handle. I know now, of course, but back then, I really wasn't sure, I figured I'd just deal with it when it came. If you'll pardon the pun.

'I licked a little off my lips, and I wasn't sure about the taste, so I wiped the rest off with my hand, and smeared it on the grass, while he just collapsed in a heap beside me, panting. It was so funny, he was completely exhausted, and it was ages before he even opened his eyes again, let alone said anything.'

'So what did he say?' Laura asked.

'I really can't remember,' Madeleine replied. 'I was too busy wondering how long it would take him to get it up again.'

'And talking of the time,' Patsy interrupted, 'I don't

101

know whether any of you ladies have noticed, but it's gone ten o'clock. So, I suggest we convene an emergency meeting of the book club for the same time next week, and maybe we can pick up where tonight's left off?'

There was a chorus of affirmatives as everybody rose, and began picking up their things.

I looked around. Pretty much the entire stock of wine had gone – there were going to be some well-toasted women rolling home this evening, and I hoped their husbands, boyfriends, partners, whoever, would be in the mood to appreciate them. I saw Madeleine nod goodbye as she went out the door, then felt a hand on my arm as another girl, Sarah, sidled over. Cute, slender, nineteen, maybe twenty. I'd never really spoken to her very often, didn't know anything about her aside from the fact she rarely had a harsh word to say about anything she read. 'A bit of a doormat,' had been Madeleine's snap summary, but I thought that maybe she was just shy. Well, tonight would surely have broken the ice for her, wouldn't it?

'Will you be back next week?' I asked.

She nodded. 'Only I don't really have a story to tell. Not that sort of story, anyway.'

Her hand was still on my arm. Interesting. I placed a hand on hers, and began walking out of the store. She didn't pull away.

'So what sort of story do you have?'

'Well, I don't even know if it'd be appropriate to tell, because there won't be any boys in it.'

'OK. So, girls?' I tried to catch her eye, but she was too quick. 'There's no girls either. Not yet, anyway.'

'So, you have a story, but no characters; you have what you think is a beginning, but no end.' Our hands were still touching on my arm. I'd never even considered she might be gay; had always assumed there'd be a Mister Mouse waiting around at home for her. Apparently not. 'Well, if you don't have any other plans tonight, maybe I might be able to help you fill in some of the blanks?'

We were almost at my car. I felt her hand twist a little to clasp my fingers. 'I'd love that ... if you'd like?'

'I'd love that too,' I told her and, as I stopped to grope for my keys in my bag with one hand, I pulled her gently toward me and kissed her. 'Very much.'

She was right. It probably wouldn't make an appropriate story for next week's book club. But one day she'll tell it to somebody, and all I have to do is make sure it's worth repeating ...

A Big So Long to Innocence
Kim Mitchell

It was a beautiful June morning, not long after my best friend had moved away, when I stepped out in the backyard in my T-shirt and shorts. I was wearing a pair of big dark sunglasses and listening to music through headphones from my iPod. It had rained during the night and the grass felt wonderful between my toes. I swept the excess water off one of the lawn chairs and lay down, closing my eyes. I don't remember how long I lay there, but the headphones were suddenly yanked from my ears.

'Hey, Butt-Fart!' Candace yelled at me. That's my sister and one of her many cute pet names for me. 'Can't you freakin' *hear*?'

'Do you *mind*?' I said.

She was in her red bikini, no doubt wanting to sunbathe, but there were two chairs, so why bug me? She was a beautiful girl, my sister, twenty years old with blonde hair and blue eyes like me, and a great body, but she has always had issues of territory and of trust, and she has always been combative in one way or another.

'What kind of music? Is it "Sesame Street" or "Hannah-freakin'-Montana"?'

I was used to her being mean to me. I sometimes felt like I wanted to hit her, but she was bigger than me, and I knew it wouldn't end up very well, so I just let it go.

'Go somewhere else so we can lie out,' Candace said.

'Who is "we"?'

Candace stepped off to the side and I saw the girl who had been standing behind her and something happened to me. I didn't know what it was. There was a warm feeling in my tummy and then tingles that ran all over me. I took off my sunglasses and stood up from the lawn chair, nearly stumbling, glad that my sister did not take the opportunity to make a joke about it.

'Jasmine, this is my little sister,' Candace said. 'Ally, this is Jasmine. Her family moved into Tara's house. Tara and Ally were best friends for a long time.'

'I'm sorry your friend moved away,' Jasmine said to me, 'and it's nice to meet you, Ally.'

Her voice was gentle like the breeze. She was about five feet and three inches tall and her skin was dark, golden-brown colored. Her hair was long and black and filled with wavy curls. She wore a yellow bikini and her body was absolute perfection with firm round breasts and a flat tummy and shapely legs, but none of that mattered much at the time as much as her face. It was her face that captured me from the start, and the way she looked at me with her beautiful dark sparkling eyes, and the way her full red lips spread into such a gentle smile.

'It's nice to meet you, too,' I said.

'I don't really want to kick you out of your own back yard,' she said.

'Oh,' Candace said, 'she doesn't *mind*, do you?'

'No, I'll be fine,' I said, and I quickly ran into the house and climbed the stairs. I went to my room and closed my door. I was breathing very heavily. I threw my iPod on my pillow and fell back across my bed. All I could think about was her face and her voice and, yes, her body did creep in there too, and what the hell was it all about? It was total confusion.

***

Three months later, I stood by the kitchen door, looking up at the clock, not knowing if I wanted it to slow down or to speed up. This day had been planned and I had followed the plan so far, and it worked. Of course, my stomach really did have a knot in it as the time approached. I saw someone through the window. It was Jasmine, wearing a yellow T-shirt and red athletic shorts. My heart began pounding …

'Hello,' she said to me, stepping in and hugging me. 'I've missed you. How are you, sweetheart?'

Jasmine's embrace was warm and secure, but I was still trembling when she let me go. I closed the kitchen door and turned around. She must have sensed my nervousness because she reached out and touched my face, caressing it softly. 'Oh, Ally, *are* you all right with this?'

'Yes,' I said.

She put one arm around my neck and leaned over me, looking into my eyes. She kissed me. She had kissed me several times over the latter part of the summer, and, although they had been sweet kisses, each kiss more passionate than the last, they had been given under much more covert circumstances. You do not want to get caught making out with your best friend's little sister. The kiss calmed me.

'Ally, I have to tell you something,' Jasmine said to me, looking down into my eyes and holding me. 'I have only been with one girl before and we didn't do much of anything, so don't feel nervous with me, OK? If you don't feel like doing anything more than talking and kissing, maybe a little touching, that's fine. I just don't want you to be scared. You're still a very young girl and you have plenty of time.'

With the last sentence, dared by the words 'very young girl', I had quickly backed away and untied my robe, allowing it to dangle open. It exposed enough to show that I was naked underneath, completely naked, and I looked to Jasmine's eyes for her reaction. What was young? I was eighteen and she was twenty-two …

'Well,' she said, 'it *looks* like you're serious.'

'I love you,' I said, 'and I want to be with you.'

I didn't know how I managed to get that out. I think it was pure guts. I knew I did desire her in that way, to touch her and be touched by her. After all, how many nights had I lain in my bed in the dark thinking about her and masturbating? There had been too many to count.

I took her hand and told her to slip her shoes off at the door. She smiled at me and took them off and then, hand in hand, I walked her to the stairs and we went up. We wound up in my bedroom, where I told her to sit on the edge of the bed. I took a deep breath and removed the robe completely. I moved close to her and watched her dark eyes move over my body.

I had very small breasts that rose in little points from my chest, and I had a very small tuft of golden pubic hair at the tip of my crack. I had a slender waist and my hips had begun to widen a bit in the past few months. My legs were not very long but they were tanned and athletic.

'You have a beautiful body, Ally,' she said. 'I want to kiss you all over.'

I let her pull me close and hold me and I leaned down and this time I kissed her. After the kiss ended, I wanted to hear her say the words, so I asked her. 'Are you in love with me, Jasmine?'

'Ally, you are very special to me, but ... give me some time.'

I kissed her again. I kissed her passionately. I wasn't disappointed. Jasmine was a dream come true, everything about her, seeing her for the first time, understanding through Jasmine what I felt about her in the beginning, and realizing she felt the same way about me.

I had been sitting in the backyard one night by myself crying quietly. Jasmine came out the back door to grab her bike and go home when she heard me there in the dark. She found me sitting in the grass and sat by me. She asked me what was wrong. I tried to tell her it was nothing, but she said, when a girl is sitting in her backyard crying, something is definitely wrong.

'Fine,' I said, 'but I can't tell anybody about it.'

'Well, maybe not your mom or your sister, but I'm impartial and non-judgmental. You can tell me anything. And I won't rat on you either.'

'No,' I said, 'I can't tell you ...'

'Well, there are some things I can't tell other people and I know how that is, Ally. It's terrible to have secrets. You know the worst one? Not being able to tell someone what you feel about *them* because you are afraid of what they might think. That's a tough one. It would be funny, you know, if both of us had that little secret, wouldn't it?'

Jasmine put her arm around me there in the grass and kissed me lingeringly on the cheek, then once again further back, closer to my ear, and I did not shrink away.

'That's my secret, Ally. I like girls. And I really like you. Can you keep my secret?'

I wiped my eyes and looked up at her, smiling. 'Yes,' I said, 'I can.'

Now, months later, I felt her lips begin to kiss me about the neck and her fingers move up and down my body. She touched my small breasts and flicked at my nipples. It caused a tickle at my throat and sent tingles straight down below.

'Why don't you come lie down?' she said.

I climbed on the bed. I was still uncertain, though this beautiful girl was doing everything to make me feel good and relaxed. I loved her kisses on my mouth, on my neck and shoulders, and lower down, finally kissing my breasts. I could feel her fingers on my thighs, and I reached up, running my fingers through those tresses of black hair. She began sucking on my nipples, getting them hard, and I realized she was breathing heavily and her crotch was half-riding my thigh. I reached out and grabbed her hips, encouraging her to grind against my thigh. She rose and grinned at me, red-faced.

'I want to see your breasts,' I said, and I watched Jasmine pull her T-shirt off over her head, then unhook her bra and take it off, showing her beautiful breasts to me. The nipples were dark, and they were already hard.

'Can I touch them?' I asked her. The question felt foolish, but she did not treat it that way.

'Please,' Jasmine said. '*Please* touch them. And play with my nipples.'

I took them in my hands, the nipples between my fingers. She continued to grind against my thigh and her movements became more and more tense. She climbed over me completely then, and she began rubbing herself against the base of my belly. I continued to pinch her nipples gently as she ground faster and faster, crying out into the quiet of the house, falling forward against me, moaning quietly and breathing heavily against my neck.

'That was beautiful. Have you ever had one of those? You know what I mean, right?' she said.

'Yes,' I told her, 'I've had them by myself.'

'Oh, I know. That was my first one with another person,' she said, kissing me. 'You know what it's called? It's called an orgasm.'

Of course I knew, but I didn't say so.

She looked down into my eyes and then lowered her mouth to my mouth, her lips caressing my lips. She did this for a long time, then slipped her tongue into my mouth and began kissing me passionately. As she did so, she lifted herself off my belly for a moment and gently pushed my legs apart, coming to rest between them.

My body was tingling everywhere as she pressed herself against me, grinding her hips. Her mouth came off of mine and she gazed down at me with a look in her dark eyes I had never seen before.

'I'm going to make love to you, baby,' Jasmine said. 'I'm going to make you come.'

'Go for it,' I said.

'I'm going to do something I've never done to a girl before, so if I do something wrong ... if it hurts, if you want me to stop –'

'Yes, Jasmine,' I said.

'Close your eyes, my sweet Ally.'

I closed my eyes and felt her warm breath on my face, her soft kisses on my cheek and then my neck, down along my throat, around to the other side of my neck. Her fingers caressed my arms and her mouth began to move along my shoulder, causing a sensation of pleasure I could not contain, and I gave off a little moan. Instinctively, I took my fingers from her hair and threw my arms around her neck as she kissed her way across my collarbone and to my other shoulder, and I moaned again, feeling her lips and tongue move along my tender flesh.

I could hear the birds chirping outside and I could feel a light breeze come in across my leg. It was getting to be the middle of the morning and the sunlight was shining in through the curtains, and I could see it on the inside of my eyelids as my lover began to kiss her way slowly further down my pubescent body. It was a beautiful day outside and it was a beautiful day inside because I was with my girl. Had I not dreamed of this day? But what had I dreamed? Kisses and embraces and, yes, perhaps to be naked with her and touch her – there was so much unknown.

Of course, now it was happening, and I did not have to worry about the unknown. She was beginning to kiss my nipples, sending that tickle to my throat and those little shocks down to my little button, and all I could do was hold on and go with what was happening. I was not afraid. My clitoris was swollen; I could feel it down there engorged like a Japanese puffer fish. Jasmine was sucking at my little red nipples, gently grazing them with her teeth. They were hard, sticking out from my little cone-shaped breasts. I opened my eyes long enough to look down at them and see Jasmine glance up at me. I rested my head back on the pillow and closed my eyes as she placed her hands on my breasts, pinching the nipples, kissing her way down my abdomen. I knew then what she was going to do. I had heard of it. I wanted her to do it.

'Excited, aren't you?' she asked me softly.

Indeed I was!

'You are beautiful,' she said, 'so beautiful and precious ...'

She continued to kiss her way down. She kissed my

tummy and came to my pussy but she did not go for that right away.

'Oh, Ally, what a *beautiful* pussy,' she said, 'but I've got to kiss those wonderful legs first.'

She nibbled my thigh and I had to take my fingers from her hair as she moved further down. She kissed her way along my leg, up the inside of my thigh, causing me to tingle all over in anticipation. Then I could feel Jasmine's fingers spreading my pussy lips. I felt her tongue touch my clitoris; she began to lick it very gently and I could feel it right down in my toes. I had nothing to compare it to, for no one had ever done it to me before, not even the few guys I had fooled around with. I was tensing my legs and ankles and flexing my toes, holding my breath and releasing it and moaning softly as the sensations grew within me. She flattened her tongue against me and began to wiggle it from side to side. The sensations in my little clitoris doubled and I reached down, locking my fingers in her hair, grinding my hips, pressing my entire vag against her mouth. I could hear her breathing hard and she grabbed my butt, cupping both cheeks. I could feel it coming. I was reaching for it. At the same time I was tensed up, trying to draw it out from force of habit. I was defeated. Jasmine's tongue flickered quickly from side to side over my clit and it was simply too much for me and I let go of her hair, threw my arms back over my head, arched my back like a girl demon-possessed and held my breath one last time. That was when I felt it, and I couldn't help but close my legs and lock Jasmine's head in a vice-grip. The cry that filled the house was my own, a wild animal-like cry that I could not have held in had I wanted to. The pleasure, the intensity of the orgasm was just too great. My butt was off the bed and I was frozen there, my clitoris pulsating against Jasmine's mouth. I was moaning and shaking and breathing hard. It was the most intense orgasm I had ever had in my life, and it wasn't ending quickly.

When it did end, Jasmine freed herself from the vice-grip of my thighs, her mouth and chin moist with my juices. I was still catching my breath.

She was pleased.

'Ally,' Jasmine said to me, 'that was so *hot*.'

'No kidding,' I said. 'I never – "came" like that before.'

'I'll say. You squirted like a quart in my mouth,' she said with a laugh. 'I swallowed.'

We lay there for a moment, snuggling quietly while I recovered, and then I rolled over on top of her and, without asking, decided I was going to return the favor. I did not really know how to go about it except to imitate what she had done, and to go with what I was feeling. I kissed her on the mouth, those beautiful lips, and then on her cheek, her neck …

I took some time to hold her breasts and suck on her hard nipples. There was something so natural and

115

beautiful about that. She moaned and ground her hips up against me. I reached down and tugged at her shorts and she lifted her butt off the bed and I stripped her completely naked. I expected to see a lot of hair, but there was not. In fact, there was just a small black strip at the top. Because she had kissed my legs all over, and because her legs were so brown and beautiful, I decided to do the same.

It was not long before I had finished the legs, though, and I was coming upon her pussy, spreading it apart with my fingers. I had looked at mine in the mirror before, and Jasmine's was different. It looked like some exotic flower: the lips were dark and perfectly shaped, and, when I spread them apart, the inside was a bright pink. Jasmine was already breathing hard with anticipation when I lowered my tongue to her sex. Her body immediately reacted to the touch. I found the hard spot high within the lips and I began to swirl my tongue against it.

'My sweet girl,' she whispered, '*that feels so good.*'

It excited me to excite her. As she began to tremble, I grasped on to her body with my fingers, wanting to feel every bit of her pleasure quake. I was riding high. I tried all different ways of licking her and found the best one so that Jasmine cried '*Yes*', clutching at my hair, grinding her hips against my face, and then grabbed the back of my head with both hands as both legs stiffened. She gasped, '*I'm coming, Ally!*' and I held on as she bucked against my face. I reached down between my own legs and rubbed excitedly. It was almost instantaneous: just as her orgasm subsided, I went off quietly.

I moved up and lay beside her. Her dark eyes looked into mine with soft passion.

'That was *something*,' she said. 'You are quite the girl.'

'So are you,' I said.

We made love again that day, and we took a bath together and washed each other, and we talked about our lives. I talked about not having a father, or not being able to remember him. I talked about how my mom treated me like her little girl, and how Candace liked to call me names and push me around. Jasmine talked about having a black father and a white mother and how some people looked at them, and how some people treated her different because she was mixed. She talked about how hard it was being different no matter what it was that was different about you. As for Candace, she didn't think I should take her treatment of me to heart. After all, we were sisters and we would be for life.

After we had aired out my bedroom, clearing it of the female fuck scents of the day, and cleaned up, I put on my nightgown and bathrobe and we spent our few last moments together in the kitchen, kissing and embracing by the door.

And she left. I closed the door and leaned against it, a warm feeling deep inside my heart. Whether it was two days or two weeks before I could be alone with her again, this day I had been in Heaven.

***

I didn't feel that tingle for another girl until a year later in college. That person was Liz, a girl in my drama class. She wasn't in my circle of friends; she was in a clique with a bunch of stuck-up girls that I could never strive to be in: sorority sisters.

After I realized it was her that made me tingly between my legs, every time after drama class I would go directly to my dorm room and masturbate. I would strip naked as I walked to the bed, flop down on it and touch myself in the sweet spot until I acquired relief from the tingling.

That was basically the whole of my freshman year as far as I can remember it. I don't remember any classes or events or any other classmates. I only remember Liz naked and then masturbating regularly about her body; I didn't even have a fantasy about being with her or what we might be doing together if we were.

That changed at the end of the second semester. The big event at the end of the year was a drama class trip to New York City. We went down on a bus on a Friday and stayed overnight then spent all of Saturday seeing sights and a Broadway show and then traveled home late Saturday night.

118

Liz and I ended up in the same hotel room and, unbelievably, in the same double bed. Two other girls were also in the room.

It took us forever to settle down. Liz and I were very quiet; I think, in retrospect, that I was so quiet that Liz figured I was asleep. I wasn't. I was hyper awake, so acutely aware that the object of so many masturbation sessions was lying next to me with just a tank-top and panties on. I wanted desperately to touch myself; I wanted to put my hand in my panties but I didn't dare get started because I'd make a bunch of noise.

I heard a little rustle next to me that might have been the back of a hand moving under a sheet and the rhythmic breathing of someone touching themselves. Just as those sounds became steady, Liz's free hand reached over and grasped my thigh. Her hand came up on to my panties and began petting my pussy through the cotton. It was electrifying. I started breathing heavily and, without hesitation but as quietly as I could, I snaked my thumbs into the elastic of my panties and pushed them down. Liz's hand hardly missed a beat, now touching my pussy lips directly. It wasn't exactly in the right place so I took the task directly in hand, no pun there, and touched myself. Our hands were rubbing together as they both worked my pussy into a frenzied froth.

Liz pulled my panties the rest of the way off my legs and pushed up my T-shirt so that it was bunched under my arms. She had done the same thing to herself and, pushing me on to my side facing away from her, she sidled her naked body up to mine and spooned me. I could feel her pussy on my butt and I wanted to start touching myself again; she held me tightly and we feel asleep.

We both woke up before the other girls and we had a minute to put ourselves together, no evidence of something dyke and wicked.

That day was so odd and painful. Liz and I didn't speak at all about what had happened. In fact, Liz didn't speak to me even once. She went back to hanging with her clique buddies and sat with them on the bus back home. It wasn't until after the last drama class for the year that she talked to me. Did I want to sleep over Friday night? she wanted to know. Her dorm mate had gone home already.

'Of course!' I blurted, although I was trying to be cool and nonchalant.

Liz put her finger up to her lips, cautioning me to silence, or at least quiet discretion, and I nodded, realizing that, just because I had been thinking about her for the entire school year, outing ourselves wasn't what she had in mind.

It seemed as if Friday would never come. I went to her room; she came to the door in a really skimpy string bikini, like a European thing, thong and just a bit of something covering her nipples. She was so beautiful.

Liz said we wanted to get to the movie she had rented to watch. She put the DVD on and we got right down to business. She started pulling clothes off. I was getting the tingly feeling between my legs in a big way. Liz pulled me on to the bed and on to her and we lay with me on top kissing and pressing our bodies together. I'd barely kissed a guy any longer than a few minutes and there were the times with Jasmine and here I was naked and really making out hot and heavy with Liz. What's funny is we had still barely even talked to one another.

Liz put her hand between my legs, fingers separating my pussy lips, and she began to finger me. My plan was to just imitate her and then I would improvise. It turns out that imitation works really well when in a situation like this. Liz *did* know what to do, and she took us through mutual masturbation and different positions for oral and even fingering each other's asshole – which I thought would be gross but when it's combined with a thumb on your clit and a couple of fingers in your cunt, it can be quite explosive.

We made love all night and slept off and on. In the morning she told me how much fun she had and hoped we could hook up again sometime. Real cool like, no words of affection or tenderness or maybe even love like I had hoped. *Hook up*.

We did the next night. Liz showed me how we could put our pussies together by intertwining our legs. It was an odd sensation at first but it got us hot and we used our hands – and fingers in our asses.

All summer I spent every moment I could jilling off, thinking about being with Liz. I had no way to reach her; she didn't give me a phone number, address or email. When I returned to college in the fall, she did not. I heard a rumor some guy got her pregnant and she married him and was living in a suburb, a normal, expected and respected life.

Mr Flint
Primula Bond

I'm already mucky, and that's just from twenty minutes sitting on the Tube. Half-moons of grime in my fingernails, a blackening rim around the cuffs and collar, and puddles all over my pointed boots. I should have learned by now that wearing snowy-white cotton around London is doomed, let alone honey-coloured suede, but I can't let my standards slip, no matter how basic the job.

Because, when I get to work, the shirt, the boots and, this morning, the tight black pencil skirt will all be coming off. I wonder what the others wear, Scruffy jeans, jogging bottoms, no doubt. Leggings. Who knows? Maybe some of them come dressed as princesses, or ice skaters. I never see them. I arrive first, and I'm done before their shift begins. I relish the peace and quiet of the very early morning, and I love to work on my own, high up in the sky suite, with no one but the dawn chorus for company.

It's still dark. I'm instructed to go up the backstairs, or use the trade lift, but sod that. I'm not walking up thirty flights, nor sharing the lift with laundry baskets stuffed with dirty napkins and stained towels. Who do they think I am?

The posh lift spits me softly into the upper echelons, where the night lights glow and London grumbles faintly down below. The workforce up here is predominantly male, and you can tell from the way they leave their work stations. Beautifully tidy, actually, apart from the odd basketball left lying around to trip me up. Female workers are far messier.

I glide through the scented silence. Think of all those City boys dozing in their glitzy apartments, sprawled across black satin sheets, some blonde stranger picked up in a bar already awake, or even tiptoeing away. Their big dicks will start rising soon, hardening against their thighs while they sleep, surging with their morning erections.

And all the while I'm preparing their little empire for them.

When all the other offices are pristine, I key in the code and the door of the presidential suite ushers me inside. This is my favourite part. This is why I come in so early. El Presidento has a glass desk the size of my kitchen, and a big white leather chair which you can swivel while you watch the sun sliding up the smooth phallic sides of the Gherkin building opposite. He obviously likes the finer things, too, as there's no sign of anything so mundane as a computer or a filing cabinet. Only a wire rubbish basket, piled with empty champagne bottles.

I put my box of utensils down and go across to the mirrored back wall. The panoramic views are reflected everywhere, and there's me, smart as any executive wife, floating in the clouds as they float past. For a minute I rule the world.

But first things first. I unbutton my overall. Sooty specks in my cleavage. I unzip my bag, and there is the packet of wipes along with my fresh pink gloves.

I spot movement outside the window. There are men jumping, no, *spraying* out of the Gherkin building as if it's a giant showerhead. Or a cock, shooting its load. Ooh, I always feel so randy at this time of the day.

The action men on the Gherkin seem, with the sunrise behind them, to be dressed all in black. They're abseiling down the curved sides. Other buildings have scaffolding or absurd cages for cleaners. Those guys do it sliding down their ropes, polishing and buffing.

I pull open my overall. I like to keep this tight, too. It accentuates my considerable curves, and helps me to concentrate. But, aah, the freedom when I'm undone. I press myself against the cool glass for a moment.

I could almost call to the abseiling men, but they're too busy to see Madame Mop, dark hair pinned up demurely, rubbing her tits against the window.

I toss my outfit across the great man's desk. Now my skin's covered in just a kiss of lace. Is that one of the men glancing over, swinging from his harness? I turn slowly, swinging my hips. The day is getting brighter. I'm sure he can see me, because his mouth is open and his wiper has stopped moving over his section. I wonder if his section's getting hard?

There's always a bit of a rush, but that gets my adrenalin pumping, the risk of discovery, the deadline before I have to vanish like Cinderella. I whisk out a wipe, sweep it between my breasts, where grubby specks have caught in the murmur of perspiration on my skin. The wipe nudges each lace cup away so that my nipples perk up. I flick each delicate point, and the cleansing fluid stings deliciously.

I do it again so that they tingle, transform from wintry pale to an engorged berry red. There's an answering twinge just inside my pussy.

Perhaps my cunt could use a clean. Hush my mouth, such language. I draw the cold wipe slowly down my stomach, over the wispy knickers I like to wear underneath my severe outfits, start to slide it over the soft crevice, but time's ticking on, I must work my magic on this office and be gone before he knows it.

The white leather chair looks so comfortable. No one will ever know if I have a twirl. The sun's swinging round. The men on the Gherkin have swung to the nether regions, and I'm alone again.

The leather creaks and caresses as I wriggle into its contours. I lift my feet on to the desk, what would the boss think if he could see me now? He doesn't even know I exist, hoovering and polishing, while on the other side of town he's standing under his shower, bubbles following the trail of hair over his stomach to his groin.

I've heard he works out. As the water sluices him he'll be lifting his big cock in that dazed, tender way men have when they're washing. He'll be thinking about the deals, the conference calls, the sackings he'll undertake when he gets in to work.

There are no trinkets on his desk, no simpering photos of a trusting wife, no rugged picture of him on a ski slope or a beach, kids or dogs. There's just a discreet trophy, a silver letter opener and a closed laptop.

And a cluster of champagne glasses from last night's party. That's good. The whole team will be hungover and even later for work. I must take the empties to the kitchenette, but my fingers are between my legs, easing under my knickers, the chair moulded around me. I swivel from side to side, sky turning blue, now towards the door, my sex lips already sticky.

The movement invites my fingers to dig deeper through the velvety folds into my warm waiting slit.

I keep it almost totally waxed apart from what my beautician calls a landing strip. Not because there's anyone around to admire it, no one begging to go down on it, but because it's cleaner. And because I'm saving myself.

I'm moist now. I draw one finger out, sniff it and the sweet salt aroma, then probe back inside. My eyes are closing as ripples of pleasure start their lazy progress, but I glance at the clock on his desk. I slide down so that my cunt is on the edge of the chair, tipped up, my legs splayed outwards while my feet grip the desk to rock me faster from side to side.

The juice'll make the chair damp. White honey on white leather. It creaks louder as I laugh to myself. If only he knew. If only his uptight secretary, perched at her computer, knew. What would she say, coming in with a pile of phone messages, to see the wet spot on her master's chair?

She wears Chanel suits and pearls, her face is inscrutable, her hair always so, her make-up discreet, no pouting red gloss which makes your mouth look like a vulva. She wears glasses with pointed frames and an expression of ice, and fantasises about his strong, powerful body under his Jermyn Street tailoring when she watches him shaking hands with important clients, peeps through his door when he's in meetings, thinks up excuses to call him when he's abroad on business.

She'd do anything for just one smile. Go down on her knees. Oh please! Imagine that, on her knees in front of him, sliding down his zipper, opening his trousers, his secret weapon thumping into her face, bold and erect, beads of spunk welling up at its tip, forcing its way through her lips ...

All I've ever had from him is an envelope of cash at Christmas.

She'd go mad to see my lustful dribble all over his precious seat. She'd know straight away what it was, because she sits on her own chair creaming herself most days. I'm almost tempted to leave it there, my bitch smell on the seat of his trousers, sharp tang of sex snaking into his nostrils every time he leans forward to sign a cheque.

Both my hands are working now. Me and the chair have a wonderful rhythm going, rock, swivel, slide, the sunshine slanting through my eyelashes as I start to gasp, my tits bouncing, the nipples rigid, I'm rubbing myself harder, opening and closing my sex, my buttocks sliding in my own sweat, heating up the leather.

Is that movement through the glass panel of the door? If anyone asks, I'm here to clean, but the ripples gather into a knot, ready to roll like a snowball.

The flash of a dark figure outside. Not one of the team already? They'd see me, writhing and moaning on the big man's white leather throne, but they wouldn't dare try to stop me –

The door is opening. Is there time for me to bring myself off, quick, I'm hanging on the edge here, my cunt twitching, my clit throbbing, the pleasure tight as wire. Just sitting here in the hot seat does it for me, up in the clouds, before the hum of life rises through the building like flame up a torch, so close, a touch on my little button will push it right over, what a show that would be for Donald and Jake come in early to take up their work stations, or Jackie or Madge come up with their dusters from the floor below to see what's going on.

'What the fuck do you think you're doing?'

I've never had a bucket of cold water thrown over me, but now I know that it would be the most ecstatic experience.

'I'm here to clean,' I moan. Far from turning me off, this great booming voice flicks all my switches. 'I've been here since dawn.'

'You're here to clean?' He strides right up to the desk, leans his fists on it gorilla-fashion and stares straight up my fanny.

'Yes, yes, Mr Flint,' I gasp, clamping my knees together and pushing myself away from the desk. He must be able to see my pussy, its slice of red silk, but at least closing my legs quells the insane quivering. 'See my gloves, over there in the bucket, and my fluids?'

There's a long pause. Not a telephone ringing, not the ding-dong of the lift. My eyes are level with his crotch. He's wearing charcoal grey with a chalk stripe, perfectly pleated.

'So when were you going to make a start?' His voice is a rasp. 'On the cleaning.'

'I assumed you'd be late.'

'I'm never late. And you're in my chair.'

Now's the time to recoup some dignity, if that's possible. My underwear barely covers the essentials. I could grab my overall and flee, or I could brazen it out. After all, he's a man of the world, isn't he? Red blood in his veins, a girl in every bank, a practically naked creature pleasuring herself in his chair like one horny Goldilocks.

You don't get to the top without a rampant libido, all that stress needs constant release, doesn't it? Didn't Kennedy need sex four or five times a day?

'What are you going to do about that, big bear?' I breathe, my voice still husky.

I sit upright, lean my elbow on the arm of his chair, stroke my chin, my mouth still open as I gasp for breath. I lower my legs, cross one over the other, swing my foot. My pussy's still burning, furious, cheated, but it's time to show what else is on offer.

I arch my back, thrusting out my tits. One strap slips down my arm. My nipples are raw with longing.

'I should call security,' he warns, and there's a definite warp in his voice. 'This office is sacrosanct.'

My eyes linger on his well-cut trousers. Is that a bulge to the left of the zip? He's standing, as leaders of industry do, with his hands on his hips, his jacket flipped out of the way. Dazzling white shirt – who irons it for him? I wonder – red silk tie, and now the craggy, handsome face.

'Oh, it's a shrine, all right. And I'd love you to call security. All those men in uniforms.' I can't believe my own cheek, but now I'm standing up. The chair knocks behind my knees. My swollen tits bounce. 'Do you think they'd frisk me?'

A crazy giggle bubbles up. I look into his eyes, grey like his suit, piercing through my insolence.

'Believe me, they're not gentle, those guys,' he answers, coming round the desk towards me. 'Especially when I give them the order.'

I can feel heat radiating out of him. I look at his mouth. There's a seam of moisture between his lips.

I sway towards him so that one breast brushes against his shirt. Warm round flesh on cool cotton, but there's a real man underneath. I'm not going to budge. Not after these years of anticipation, wondering what he would be like up close like this, isolated from his colleagues and clients.

He doesn't flinch. His breath blows on my forehead, raising a sweaty strand of hair. I can smell his cologne. What was he thinking about as he patted it on this morning, gazing out over London?

'They can manhandle me all they like,' I say, throwing caution to the winds. The marigolds and the J cloths will have to wait. 'But I'm not going to let you slip through my fingers.'

'Not had a good rogering for a while? All dried up? You have to get your kicks from the boss's seat?' he growls, turning me as if in a slow dance.

The glass edge of the desk digs into my butt, nice pain, and I focus on a greying lock of his hair falling over one eyebrow. Cruel words, but the gamble has paid off, because he can't keep those steely eyes off the thrust of my tits.

'So sack me.'

I daresay he can be a bully in the boardroom, his features stony with stress, but how many of them have penetrated the inner sanctum? Or, should I say, had him penetrate their inner sanctums?

I can see lust sparking in his eyes, a flush infusing his face and, best of all, he shifts his weight towards my body, not away. That's enough encouragement for me.

He glances over at the door. The entire department can peer through, if they want to, but they wouldn't dare barge in. I catch his distraction and rub my damp fanny against his trousers. There it is. The blunt instrument, hard and ready. Exquisite tailoring, to hide it so well. Does anyone else ever notice or wonder how big it is, how good it is, as they dawdle by the water cooler?

No point pretending I'll be cleaning this morning. He looks as if he's about to give me a good caning. Oh, this scenario is making me so wicked. There's only one thing to do about it now he's here.

133

'I'll decide whether writhing about on the presidential chair is a sacking offence or not. But, while I ponder the matter, I'd like it back.'

He lets go of my arms and sinks into the white leather. There's shadow on his cheeks and chin. He looks dark against the white, his eyes glittering.

The lift bell dings. A big square of sun is advancing across the carpet. Over the top of his head I can see myself in the vast mirror. Hair curling down from the pins, eyes without the spectacles big and crazy, tits huge and dominant.

'And while you're pondering, Mr Flint, why don't you fuck me?'

I've come all this way, waited this long to take what anyone else could only dream of. I straddle him, lower my crotch, slide myself up his long legs until I'm in his lap, and the length of his cock is nudging against my slit. I let it rest there for a minute, relishing the promise. Let him push me off if he doesn't want what I'm offering.

But he doesn't move. He has astonishingly long lashes, I notice, and his eyelids are relaxing very slightly. He'd never show the transatlantic team even the slightest weakness, would he? But here he is, dissolving into a pure human.

I raise my arms to unpin my hair. My breasts are inviting white mounds in the daylight, punctuated by those tight red berries, enticing him to touch. There's a taut moment when all I can hear is our harsh breathing, then with a grunt he starts to caress my breasts, flicking the acorn-hard nipples idly through the slippery silk.

The reaction sizzles instantly through me so that I jerk my hips, opening myself against the rigid shape of his cock, while he, smooth operator that he is – how many women has he undressed in his time? – easily unclips my bra so that my tits bounce freely into his face and he catches one, bites the nipple, no preamble. I rise on my knees, always worshipping, and grip the back of the chair so his face is forced against me, his mouth wrapped round the aching bud.

I arch and stretch, desire crawling through me as he bites and sucks, and I'd willingly freeze this moment, but I can't wait to see his majestic prick in all its glory. I get at his zip, wait for him to stop me, but, although he pauses, there's little he can do, and now I'm easing the solid length down from its upright position, clamping my fingers around it, taking it prisoner.

My pussy is yearning towards it, twitching to kiss and swallow it, the damp curls tangled with moisture as I hover over him, and still he's licking each stiff nipple and there's an urgency in me, that knot is tight and growing.

I start to sink, my legs giving way, raking my hands through his hair. I thought it would be wiry, but it's soft, mostly dark, only grey round the temples. The urge to grind myself on to him is overpowering.

'Who would have thought it?' he groans, muffled by my soft flesh. 'Mrs Overall, a secret temptress –'

Why didn't I do this years ago? Walk into his office, strip off and sit on his face? See, they're all the same underneath the wrapping. Although he's more magnificent than most. To find out, I rest on the rounded tip of his knob, letting it nudge blindly just inside my crack, setting fire to that most sensitive part of me, but now, although I'm loving the sharp delight of his teeth on my nipples, I want to look at him while this happens.

'Admit it. You never notice the uniform, let alone the underling inside it,' I chide, holding his face between my hands as I rock, letting his knob tease my burning clit, no further inside, just tickle the surface, prepare me, use him like a toy before I lower myself on to him, down that long thick shaft. The smooth surface is already damp from where I've slicked it with my honey, and that shoots stronger thrills of excitement through me.

'I'm a busy man.'

'Not too busy for some morning delight, Mr Flint.' I close my eyes for a moment. I intend to have many more mornings like this. 'Let me show you how it's done.'

I grind down hard, no more messing, and his cock makes contact with the burning nub of my clit. My brave words die in a filthy sigh as I savour the pulsating length fitting hard inside me, a hot beast filling me, attached to the man everyone admires, impaling myself on him. I pause, my tits nudging his face as he watches me.

'I'm never too busy for the right woman,' he murmurs, tightening his grip on my hips as I reach the base of his cock and we wait for the rhythm to begin.

'Well, you've found the right woman now.'

I can't wait any longer. I start to stroke up and down his cock as it goes on growing inside me, no choice but to move, engulf him, every inch of him grazing every screaming inch of me so that I can only go so far before slamming back down on him, groin on groin, and each time I do it his knob is as hard as rock.

'What's the rush?' He grabs my hips to slow me down. 'Now that we're here. You'll go as fast as I tell you.'

He settles against the chair but I'm not fooled because he's not slacking, far from it, next thing he's slamming right up inside me and, when we start to collide, over and over, my triumphant moans rise in a wild crescendo.

He's harder, I'm wetter, rivulets of fire streak up me, my breasts bounce frantically, his eyes watch, teeth gritted, as I'm curving and arching, trying to curb the inevitable, but it's flooding through me and his eyes are glazing over, still trained on me and my body bucking on to him, and then it peaks and floods, my climax, up here on the top floor, astride the top dog, and the most incredible thing of all is that he's not gritting his teeth, the top dog is smiling.

No one's ever seen him smile, his lips are curling not in their habitual snarl but a real splitting grin of pleasure and triumph as he pumps his spunk into me, throwing me upwards with the force of his climax as I fail to bite back my screams.

'What have I told you about keeping perfect silence in my office?' he mutters into my hair, pulling me across him so my tight body can milk his dying erection. 'Can't have any distractions from world domination, you know –'

'Speak when you're spoken to, Mr Flint,' I whisper, rising and falling on his chest.

I wasn't imagining those sounds. There are barely muffled voices whispering and tittering outside the door. With a sly chuckle, Mr Flint heaves me off him, packing away his subsiding cock and zipping up his trousers.

I slide back into the white leather chair, leg hooked over the arm, totally sated, already lusting for more of him as he marches across the room, wags his fingers at the prying faces outside and rattles down the blind.

And as for the marigolds? Well, perhaps in time he'll learn to love the feel of rubber on his skin.

The Method
Justine Elyot

'You're so easy to fuck.'

I laughed when Gabe said this to me, principally because he had never fucked me in his life. All the same, we were sitting up in a rumpled bed, half-naked, me wearing a bra because of the bizarre no-nipple ruling by the TV channel who funded the series. I mean, who the hell would actually shag with a bra on? Ridiculous and uncomfortable.

So our circumstances might have looked as if they justified his comment. But the reality was that a brief but fierce rubbing together of his boxers and my boy shorts was the closest we had come to actual congress – and all of that done in front of a crowd of guys in hoodies with cameras and clipboards. Not the most erotic atmosphere in the world.

Besides, I hardly knew Gabe. I don't know if it was the director Lynsey's idea of a joke to make the sex scene first on the filming schedule, but our characters didn't get to formally 'meet' each other until week three. I knew Gabe from his work, of course, which was very much in the heart-throb hero vein, but that was all.

So it was surreal to find ourselves stripping off after the most cursory of introductions and diving into bed together.

'Thanks,' I said, conscious of his animal warmth and male smell right up next to me. It was making me a bit giddy, to be honest. It had been a while since I sat in bed beside an attractive man. 'I feel like I ought to have a cigarette. And what do you mean, easy to fuck? Compared to whom?'

His lip curled roguishly. 'All of them. For a start, all the younger ones spend an hour obsessing over which bits of their body they want picked up on camera before we even get down. They don't ever pay *me* any attention. I'm just an accessory, really, a foil. Something to make them look even better.'

'They're vain, you mean?'

'Exceptionally. Mind you, so am I.' He shrugged. 'Two vain gits going at it don't generate that much heat, I've found. Whereas you, well, you're different. Something about you that's earthier, unforced.'

'Hmm.' Not sure this was a compliment, I sucked in my imaginary cigarette smoke and waited for him to elaborate.

'I'm trying to work out if your sexual energy comes from your character or from you. Because right now, I'm finding you alarmingly sexy, and I really never expected to.'

A strange admission, but hardly a surprising one. He was twelve years younger than me and the up-and-coming stud of his generation. I was at that stage in my career when I got picked for 'real women' roles. All the minxy man-magnet stuff was well in the past. Which was good, because I got to act at last, but then again ...

'Well, my character fancies your character, even though she knows there's something not quite right about him. I think that sense of knowing she's taking a risk but taking it anyway makes it hotter for her.'

'And you?'

'Gabe, darling, you're a pretty face, I won't deny. But I'm long past that stage.'

'What stage?'

'Oh, you know. All the extra-curricular activity.'

'What, having sex?' Gabe's bright-blue eyes were amused, challenging me. I began to feel a creepy, pins and needly sensation around the pit of my stomach. Was I actually attracted to him? 'You're past fancying someone and going to bed with them? Christ, Kate, that's the saddest thing I ever heard. What a waste.'

I found myself wondering what DI McLeish would say to this. Something robust and ballsy, yet with that undercurrent of vulnerability that made the character come to life, no doubt. Really, the show was a tired rip-off of *Prime Suspect*, but it seemed to be popular with the audience, so we plodded on, year after year. It was a fantastic pension plan, if nothing else.

'One night stands just don't do it for me any more, Gabe,' I told him. 'Me and my vagina deserve something with a bit more quality and endurance.' Like my vibrator, though I didn't say that.

'Who said anything about a one-night stand?'

'Gabe, are you sexually harassing me in my workplace?'

He chuckled. 'I guess I am. Sorry. Look, why don't we go and get a drink after this? Talk through our character dynamic in a bit more detail. I've never played a villain before, and I'd value your advice.'

'Well, I can't say I've played a serial killer before. But why not? OK.'

Marvellous, isn't it, how the sexy serial killer has become a trope. Gabe is the latest in an ever-growing line of them. He was cast because of his astonishingly blue eyes. Apparently, they make it easy for people to believe that he might be a psychopath.

'So, are you a psychopath?' I asked him, over red wine in the hotel bar, once we were dressed and released from the studio.

'Of course not.' He gave me a strange look.

'It's just those baby blues, you know. So intense. You just have to be.'

He laughed, cottoning on. 'Silly, really, isn't it? I've got mad staring eyes so I look like a killer. You're over forty with a sharp haircut so you must be a ballbusting bitch.'

'Touché,' I said, with a rueful sip of the wine. 'And ouch.'

'No, I don't mean you *are*.' His rush to self-justification cheered me. 'I mean, that's the cliché, isn't it? I know you aren't really.'

'How do you know? How do you know I'm not a ballbusting bitch?'

'Because of the way you were in bed.'

'What? You judge my character on a few wriggles and writhes for the camera?'

'No, there was more to it than that.'

I made a move away, as if to refute him, but he caught hold of my wrist, pre-empting me. I was forced to look into those chiller killer eyes.

'Wasn't there?' His voice was so soft. The way he said it made me squirm and feel an unwelcome wetness at my crotch.

'DI McLeish needed to get close to Ryan on an emotional level. She needed to make the experience as intense for him as it was for her.' But I was babbling and he knew it.

'I'm not talking about McLeish and Ryan. I'm talking about Kate and Gabe.'

'I don't know you.'

'Do you want to?'

My blood was roaring in my ears. Danger was all around me, danger in the form of his kissable lips and his cheekbones and his smouldering-for-England eyes. That was before you even got to his body, which he appeared to have stolen from a catalogue model.

Yes, he was hot, he was flirting with me, he was sexy as hell, but was he safe?

'Look, this is a bit weird. I don't get young studs coming on to me that much. You are coming on to me, aren't you?'

'Oh yes,' he said.

'Tell me more, doctor Gabe, about this analysis you've done on the basis of my TV frolicking? What did you find out about me?'

He leaned into me, so that our shoulders touched, and took the wineglass from my hand. Once he'd placed it on the table, he turned his head so that his lips were so close to my ear that his breath tickled my skin.

'There was this moment,' he whispered, 'when I pinned your wrists, and your eyes went all far away, like you were in your deepest, most secret, happiest place. You probably don't know you did it, but you arched your back, just a little bit, and pushed yourself right up against me. It was so instinctive, and so fucking sexy. God, I wanted to have you right there. I didn't hear what Lynsey was saying. I think we might have to retake the scene because I wasn't paying attention to anything but your sweet, wet pussy and that look on your face.'

I wanted to speak, but my throat had closed up.

When words stuttered out, they were hoarse. 'I noticed you were hard. Thought it was just an occupational hazard.'

'I was hard for you, Kate. I want you. And I think you need what I can give you.'

'You're an arrogant cock, aren't you?'

'You like that. That's the thing that turns you on. That, and being pinned down. I can pin you down, Kate. I can pin you down morning, noon and night.'

'Yeah, but what if you turn out like Ryan? What if you're a serial killer?'

'Take the risk.'

'I've taken risks before. They didn't pay off.'

'All you're risking is a bad shag, and I'm promising you it won't be.'

In my hotel room, he lived up to his promise.

It felt subversive and surreal to be standing between his thighs as he sat on the bed, examining every inch of me with the ray-gun beam of his eyes. This was a man who could be shagging a different exquisite starlet every night of the week, and yet he was with me.

'I first saw you in *Jail Birds*,' he said, running his hands over my hips in their tight skirt.

'Christ, you must have still been at school! Why did your parents let you watch that?'

'Oh, they never had a clue what I was doing. They were probably out swinging or something. Anyway. You were fucking hot in that. That scene in the shower with that sexy drug-dealer girl … phew. Fuelled my fantasies for a long, long time.'

'Oh, God.' It seemed wrong to laugh, but the thought of the tender young Gabe lying in his bed picturing me in that classic of trash TV was too much. 'How embarrassing.'

'Why embarrassing? You're a goddess, Kate. You were then and you are now.'

'Your silver tongue will get you into trouble one day.'

'I hope so. I like trouble.'

Suddenly he yanked me down so I fell heavily on the bed beside him. Before I knew it, his mouth was on mine, for the second time that day. I knew how he would taste, but the kiss wasn't the same as the one we'd shared on set. We'd been doing that by numbers. Things had been running through my head, things like *Remember to communicate urgency, passion, abandonment. Remember what's at stake for McLeish. Show the audience that you are in deeper than you want to be.*

But now it was *Urgency, passion, abandonment. There's a lot at stake for me. I'm in deeper than I want to be.*

Then all that was swept away by his tongue, by his skin, by his scent, by the endless greedy investigation of my body by his hands. He broke my skirt zipper but I didn't care, just wanted it off so he could get at my thighs, my bottom, my cunt. The silky shirt came off much more easily, and my bra was not going to feature in this sex scene. It found itself in very short order flung across the bedroom, leaving my breasts free to be squeezed and fondled by Gabe's expert hands.

He felt so perfect, I wanted to devour him. Firm flesh, strong arms, flat stomach, long legs. I wanted all of it, on me and in me. I kissed him all over his face and neck, and he returned the gesture, nipping at me with sharp little teeth, so I knew he was ravenous too.

He had invitingly pink nipples, so I nibbled on them until he stopped me with a good echoey smack to my bum and growled, 'Get on your back.'

I rolled over, my pussy tingling at the way he issued the order, and looked up at him. He did look unnervingly like a killer trying to work out where he was going to stab me. His brow was low, his lips in a grim straight line. Calculations were taking place. I put my arms over my head, a gesture of surrender designed to soften him.

I might have been self-conscious about my age, but I was confident that I still had a good body, gym-firm and supple. If Gabe wanted to twist me into yoga configurations, he would have no trouble from my joints.

'How long has it been, Kate?' he whispered, looking down at my supplicant pose.

'Too long. Look, are you going to fuck me or shall we just talk about it?'

'Oh, feisty and hardboiled, just like McLeish. Are you in role?'

'No, I'm on heat. Get on with it.'

He made a shushing sound, pretending to disapprove, though I could tell he was tickled. I braced myself, expecting him to climb aboard and spear me, once the condom thing was dealt with, but he surprised me by making a dive for my crotch and pushing his face into it.

I had expected more enthusiasm than technique, but he had championship quantities of both, and he nibbled and licked, sucked and tongued until I could take no more, resentful of the fact that he had made me come before I'd had the chance to bring him to his knees. It seemed unequal somehow. I was meant to be the femme fatale, the Mrs Robinson, not the quivering, whimpering thing he'd made me.

I was angry with him, bizarrely, ungratefully, and I pushed him down and grabbed his cock, still inside his trousers but not for long.

'Whoa there,' he exclaimed. 'Didn't you like that?'

'Oh, I liked it all right.' I wrestled his erection out of its coverings and pushed down the trousers. 'But I'm exploring my motivation. Which is that I find you very attractive and I want to eat you up.'

'That's a good motivation,' he remarked before gasping,

as I cupped his balls and took half of his length in my mouth for a first good suck.

I teased him, then satisfied him, alternating flickers and licks of the tongue with full, luxurious mouthfuls of his cock, pumping its base with my hand, while his fists clenched and unclenched helplessly on the sheets.

Now I had him, the over-confident young buck, at my mercy.

As his little cries gathered in urgency and his nails began to drag at the cotton, I sensed that the time was right to ... remove his cock from my mouth and scoot backwards, away from him.

'What? Don't you ... dare ...' He was all confusion, all tousled, sweaty, disbelief.

I laughed at him.

He lunged.

We chased each other around the bed in a mock-battle of swiping limbs until he pounced, pinning me as he had promised he would, just like his character pinned McLeish.

The condom came out and he didn't risk giving me the freedom to elude him again, keeping my wrists in his grasp until he was safely lined up and ready to push his way inside me.

'What's your motivation now?' he asked, nudging my cunt tantalisingly without ever slipping in. 'Eh?'

'Lust,' I told him. 'The same as yours.'

He rewarded me with penetration, a quick and easy dash to the hilt.

'Let's turn motivation to action.'

Action, not acting, became the force that drove us. His cock was in my cunt; there was no room for interpretation there. Sincere thrusting, gripping, flexing of muscles, grunting, physical and sensual greed overtook our minds. Our brittle sophistication was gone and we were all animal need.

Afterwards, lying in his arms, I took a call from Lynsey.

'Look,' she said, 'I hate to mess you around, but that scene wasn't quite right. You were perfect, but he ignored a couple of directions. Could we re-shoot tomorrow?'

Gabe, whose phone was switched off, had a smile on his face that meant trouble. 'Told you,' he whispered.

Once I'd ended the call, he huddled a little bit closer and spoke into my ear. 'I dare you to do it for real tomorrow.'

'What? Have actual sex? On camera?'

'Go on. Why not? It'll turn into one of those urban myths. Did they or didn't they? There'll be a page about us on Snopes.'

'It'll just be something for you to dine out on for years. I shagged Kate Baxter for real on camera. No thanks.'

'I wouldn't do that. I don't want you as some kind of trophy. That's not what this is about. Is that what you think it's about?'

I sighed. 'I don't know what to think. This doesn't happen to me a whole lot.'

'I get a vibe from you that's real. That isn't, "Ooh, you're a hot superstar milf, I want to shag you". It's more, "I don't want to shag you but I can't help myself". That's what's so fucking irresistible about you. That's what makes me want you more than anything.'

His words, intense as they were, seemed heartfelt.

'And,' he added, 'think what it would add to the scene.'

I laughed out loud. 'Sometimes you can take method acting too far, you know.'

He winked at me. 'I disagree.'

***

So it was that we found ourselves the next morning wrapped in dressing gowns, jittering on a chilly set, waiting for the lighting to warm up and the cameras to find the right positions. We sipped from plastic cups of coffee, trying to look relaxed and professional. Gabe made some lame jokes. I had aching legs from shagging all night – from time to time they felt shaky.

'OK,' said Lynsey from her chair. 'Everything you did yesterday was brilliant until you got under the covers and Gabe missed a couple of cues. So if you get into bed and start with the kissing bit ...'

It was easy enough for me to slip into bed and discard the dressing gown over the side. I was wearing that stupid bra, but I also had to wear knickers for the purposes of post-shoot recovery. This might be awkward, but I figured Gabe could find a way.

Gabe, when he got beneath the sheets, had to adjust the waistband of his boxers before rolling on top of me. I felt his pre-rubbered cock spring up and rest itself on my stomach, then slide right down over my pubic bone until it dug into the crease of my thigh.

The kiss, when it started, was hotter and more fervent than yesterday's. Gabe was already well on his way, his tongue curling around mine. While we worked on keeping everything above the sheets visible to camera, what was going on beneath them was a different story.

Gabe's hand, the one that wasn't pinning my wrists, reached downward, a slow, smooth progress that aimed to rumple the sheet as little as possible. It followed the contour of my side at first, gliding down, then crossing my pubic triangle and resting in between my thighs.

He had already parted them, placing his legs squarely inside, and the shallow basin between our groins made a perfect hiding place for his wicked hand. His knuckles rubbed against my knickers, easing open my lower lips. He'd be able to feel the dampness there, I thought, kissing on, angling my head so the camera would pick up the misty longing in my eyes and all that.

'Break the kiss,' said Lynsey. 'Intense eye contact now, and it ought to be clear that you are having sex.'

I expected it was clear that we were having sex, because Gabe had pulled aside my knickers and guided his thick cock inside. I lifted my hips, just as I had done without even knowing it the day before, and let him slide deep.

We were doing it. He was fully inside me and we were fucking on camera.

Now we had to play this carefully, so nothing of the truth was revealed. With my unpinned hand, I made sure I held the sheet so it couldn't rise up off the mattress and give anyone an unexpected exhibition.

Gabe kept his moves slow and fluid. I thought he was holding his breath. It was weird, having to look into his eyes passionately when it was very obvious that the pair of us were bursting with guilty arousal.

His hidden fingers went to my clit, circling it with devilish efficacy. Suddenly, the flaw in the plan became clear to me. While it might be amusing and naughty to fuck on camera, I didn't want to come! Not in front of all these people. I wasn't sure my real orgasm was anything like my faked one in terms of quality.

For TV, because I knew it would be dubbed, I didn't usually let out a sound during sex scenes, just looked as if I was gasping, screwed my eyes shut, floundered around for a bit. In reality, I always made a hell of a racket.

As for Gabe, surely he would have to hold himself

back? Otherwise he was stuck with a used condom to dispose of and no obvious place to put it.

I tried to clamp shut my thighs, but it was too late. He had his strong legs firmly ensconced between them. I thought about risking repurposing the hand that was holding the sheet and trying to tug Gabe's fingers out of my pussy lips, but figured that opened us up to the danger of full exposure.

There was nothing I could do. I was halfway to heaven and a lot closer to the end of my career.

'OK, let's have the look of ecstasy,' drawled Lynsey.

I exhaled noisy relief. We wouldn't have to end this before we ... ended it.

I heard Gabe click his tongue very slightly, clearly frustrated, but he did as Lynsey said and began to hammer away, faking pained facial contortions while I did the eyelash-fluttering bliss.

Just as we were about to finish, he did something utterly fiendish.

He unpinned my wrists and, making it look like an accident, managed to catch his watch in my bra cup and wrench it down over my nipple.

'Oh, Gabe!' yelled Lynsey. 'You plank! We'll have to redo the whole thing.'

I kneed him quite sharply and, while he recoiled, I asked if we couldn't just do the ending.

'We had the lot in one smooth take,' said Lynsey. 'It

was so good. OK, I guess we can use the first bit and edit on the ending. Go from where he speeds up, yeah?'

'I'm going to kill you,' I informed Gabe into his ear, while he grinned down at me and gave his cock a little circular wiggle inside.

'I just didn't want to end,' he whispered. 'Not yet.'

He kept his fingers on my clit, working them harder and harder. He contrived to spoil the orgasm bit four times in total. By the time we got to the fifth take, well … let's just say my acting … wasn't.

I managed to keep my voice down by muffling it in Gabe's chest. His fingers pressed into the juices that gushed out of me, while his cock worked hard to get to the same conclusion, but, alas, he'd run out of blooper ideas and the scene had to end before he did. I know the flush on my face must have been very obvious to the crew, as was my shaky demeanour and excessive thirst afterwards. I did derive some satisfaction from knowing that Gabe had to spend the rest of the morning's filming still erect and rubbered up, with no chance of relief until he was able to bundle me into the dressing rooms during the lunch break.

There was some discussion, you might recall, in the newspaper reviews about the sex scene. Rumours abounded on the internet, and they still do. McLeish collars her killer in the end – to use the jargon – but our relationship soon became a staple of the gossip columns.

So – did they or didn't they? Only we knew, until now. It's still our favourite scene together, one we have watched and rewatched over and over again. And I'm sure we will continue to do so.

Keeping a Promise
Jenny Swallows

My hand was on Barry's crotch, my fingers tight around the bulge that pressed against the fabric of his trousers. But I barely remembered they were there, as my mind focused instead on the taunting shivers that swept through my body, as his own fingers traced up and down my moist slit, parting my lips with the gentlest touch, and sending my heart rate into orbit.

I ended a kiss that had lasted forever, and looked down, fumbling with his zipper – no, my mistake, buttons. But I'd scarcely moved before his free hand slipped on to the back of my head and, with a loud, almost rapturous groan, he angled it in the direction of his lap. Angled and pushed.

I broke his grip. 'What are you doing?'

His eyes met mine and I was surprised by the look of absolute horror on his face. 'I'm sorry, I thought you were going to ...' His voice trailed off, shocked into silence, I think, by the way my eyebrows raised as he spoke.

I kissed him. 'Sorry, no.' A pause, and then, 'I don't like doing that.'

The horror turned to hurt. 'No, of course you don't. I'm sorry, I don't know what came over me.'

I gave him my sweetest smile. 'Well, perhaps you'd better come over me instead.' I finally unfastened that recalcitrant fly and slid my hand gently in to grasp him. So hard, so warm; as my fingers closed around him, I could feel his pulse beating like a drum. My thumb ranged over his helmet, gliding through the pre-come that coated the flesh, teasing at the eyelet from whence it came.

I glanced down. My hand looked tiny against his shaft. My nostrils caught his scent, as thick as his prick. One little kiss – that wouldn't hurt, would it? But no. I'd made myself a promise and, no matter how stupid it sounded, I intended keeping it. Besides, there was no time. I'd only just begun jerking him when I felt his body tense, heard his breath catch in his throat, and then his cock jerked so hard that, for a moment, I thought I'd broken it off.

His come was thick and almost blindingly white. It didn't spurt, it erupted, a great glob of cream that rose above his swollen glans, hung for a moment as though inspecting its domain, and then fell hot and heavy on to my still-stroking hand. Again, I almost forgot myself; almost gave in to the urge to lean hungrily forward and take him into my mouth, to savor the last few drops of his ecstasy, and feel him softening between my lips.

But I caught myself before I moved and contented myself with a few gentle squeezes, before looking around for a tissue. Typical bachelor's apartment, there wasn't one in sight. I wiped my hand on his belly instead, then kissed him once again. 'There, wasn't that a lot better?'

Barry rested his forehead against mine. 'That was amazing. Thank you.' And that's what I love about guys. It doesn't matter how much they beg and plead for you to do some special thing for them, once they've come, it really doesn't matter. Who says romance is dead?

***

You know how sometimes you get an idea into your head, and it won't go away, no matter how hard you try to shake it? On the subway to the office, sitting at my desk, during the dull parts of staff meetings, lying in bed at night – *especially* lying in bed at night, the thing was spiraling around in my mind until my nipples burned and my pussy flooded. Written down like that, it sounds like it was the only thing I thought about … but then who am I trying to kid? It was. I don't think I've masturbated so much since I was a teenager.

My friend Sandra started it, eight-plus months pregnant, and having a last night out before her life became subsumed beneath a tidal wave of diapers, rattles and baby talk. We were sitting – or, rather, I was sitting; she was perched uncomfortably on the edge of the sofa – in my living room, just talking about the same sort of things we always talked about when we got together. Work, other women, and sex. Right now we were on to sex.

'So how's Mike adjusted to things?' I asked, nodding towards her swollen belly.

'However I tell him to.' She smiled, but there was a hard truth to her words, despite the jocularity. No one ever asked who wore the figurative trousers in Sandra's home, and I very much doubted whether things had changed now. 'I'll tell you what, though. He said the weirdest thing the other night ...'

I laughed. Mike often said weird things. For Sandra to actually remember one, though, it had to be a real doozy.

'We were messing around, I was telling him what a pain it was having to use the breast pump all the time, so he started ... well, you know ...'

'Feeding?' I prompted.

'I don't think that was his actual intention. He was just playing with my nipples, this thing with his tongue that he knows I like. But he got one helluva mouthful. It was hilarious, the look on his face, the coughing and spluttering ...'

I opened my mouth to speak, but she hushed me. 'I know exactly what you're going to say. The thing is, that's what he said as well. Well, not exactly, but along the same lines. "That must be what it's like to suck off a cock" is what he said. And then, and this is the weird bit, "I've often wanted to ask you what it feels like".'

'Did you ask him why he hadn't?'

'I think I was too surprised. I didn't know guys even thought about things like that!'

You know, I don't think I had, either. But, from then on, that's all I could think about, the fact that there must be thousands of guys who have wondered the same thing, and that sent the thought-train chuffing even further forward, to wonder whether guys have any idea whatsoever, precisely what it means to a girl when she takes a mouthful of hot come?

What is going through her mind as it floods her throat and she fights against choking? As her taste buds struggle to absorb the strange, new flavor (because it does taste different, almost every time)? As her body struggles against the instinct to spit, not swallow? Could a man even begin to comprehend the manner in which all those sensations and emotions merge together into one unmissable surge of animal lust, greed and triumph? And, even more intriguingly, was there any way of letting them in on the secret?

It was that thought, more than any of the others, that kept my mind whirling as I tried to sleep. Well, there was only one way to find out.

Barry probably wasn't the guy I should be trying this

on, though. We'd been seeing one another for almost a month and, believe it or not, last night was the closest we'd ever come to sleeping together, a bout of heavy petting and a come stain on his cushions.

Of course, I probably wasn't helping things along. Almost a month, and the most he'd got out of me was a grope and a handjob. Oh, and the assurance that, if he was looking for blowjobs, he'd better not start waving it in my face. I mimicked myself in my mind. 'I'm sorry, I don't like doing that.' Some guys would have spent the rest of the evening trying to convince me I was wrong; others would have lost their boner on the spot, and sent me packing into the night – yes, I've heard all the stories.

Barry, though, just took me at my word and, when he called this morning to check our arrangements for this evening – a spin around the antique stores, and then a late downtown dinner – there wasn't even a hint of reproach in his voice. Wow, a gentleman, at last. Plus, if it didn't work out between us, I knew just the gal to introduce him to. Sally really *didn't* like doing it.

Ah, but it would work out, because I had a plan. Or, at least, I would have, once I'd figured out what it was. I just hoped he'd stick around long enough for me to put it into action. Like they say in those advertisements for snake-oil – sorry, for Male Enhancement products – I'd have him feeling like he was eighteen again.

As I changed my clothes after work, I ran through the

options that presented themselves. I did not want him sucking a real cock. Or a fake one, come to that. I wasn't certain quite where our relationship was going, or even where I wanted it to go. But anything that happened between us needed to be natural, unforced, spontaneous. It needed to be between the two of us alone. And it needed to be his idea.

* * *

'Dinner was lovely, thanks.' I kissed him and looked expectantly up the street, as though a taxi would magically materialize there and then. A glance at the clock across the road could have told me that it wouldn't – a few minutes past eleven on a Friday night, every cabbie in the city would be plying his trade in the theater district, four blocks in the other direction.

'We might be in for a wait.' Barry shrugged, and I could sense the apology forming on his lips.

'Fancy a walk, then?' I asked brightly. 'It's still early and it's only –' I counted quickly in my mind '– half a dozen blocks to my place. You can always call for a cab home from there.' I thanked heaven he didn't have his cell with him.

'If you don't mind. We're not in the best of neighborhoods.' I saw his eyes sweep the arcades and Triple X video stores that lined both sides of the street.

'I walk it all the time,' I assured him, and slipped an arm through his. 'Besides, if the White Slave Trade should leap out, I'll tell them you're already spoken for.'

We started walking, slower than I think he felt comfortable with, and slowly enough, too, that every garish window display that we passed seemed to take an eternity to slip out of view. And I could see him absorb every one, through the corner of his eye.

We chatted about our plans for the weekend. Barry was seeing his kids the following afternoon and evening; maybe we could get together on Sunday?

I agreed delightedly. 'I'll cook, if you like.' And then, stopping suddenly, 'Maybe we should rent some videos?'

He looked at me; then turned around, to gaze – I assume in bewilderment – at the storefront behind him. Pirate Cove Video.

I laughed. 'Not from here, silly. Unless you want to?'

He shook his head. 'No, sorry. I knew what you meant. It was just that your timing was a little off.'

Yeah, sure it was. I stepped to the window. Pirate Cove's great; years ago, when the local authorities used to make up the obscenity laws as they went along, Pirate Cove was the only store that managed to stay in business, battling the city every step of the way, always making sure that their window displays were so close to the letter of the law that you couldn't have slipped a dollar bill through the gap. They were busted so many times that people used to joke that the only people who worked there were lawyers and undercover cops – and then it turned out that it wasn't a joke after all, because the store was actually owned by a civil liberties lawyer, for whom the fight was less of a crusade than it was a hobby.

The display tonight wasn't one of their best, but I pulled Barry alongside beside me. 'See anything you fancy?'

'You are on form tonight, aren't you?' He chuckled and wrapped an arm around me. 'How about if you tell me whether there's anything you fancy?'

Actually, there wasn't. Bondage and submission were the dominant themes and, while there was a lot else going on around the whips and chains and full-face leather masks, it seemed gratuitous to physically point them out. I peered deeper into the store, reading the handful of signs that marked the display cases. 'What do you think bukkake is?'

I heard Barry splutter. 'It's ... I don't know. I don't think you'd like it, though.'

I squeezed his arm. 'You're the boss. How about, oh, I don't know. Maybe we should just watch television instead.'

He nodded, and was that a shadow that crossed his face, or a cloud of disappointment? As we started walking again, I hoped it was the latter.

It turned out I'd miscalculated when I told him how

far we'd be walking. It was closer to nine blocks than six back to my place and, by the time we arrived there, I was beginning to hope that he would just call for a cab, and let me fall straight into bed. But his arms encircled me as I hunted for my key and, as we kissed on the doorstep, the urgency with which his hips pressed against me let me know that, if I sent him home tonight, we'd both be regretting it tomorrow.

I pushed the door open and, as I stepped inside, he whirled me around and buried his face in my neck, his mouth hot and wet against my flesh. I slipped a hand under his jacket and tugged at his shirt. It untucked easily, and I let my fingertips graze his bare back.

His hand was on my breast, pawing roughly at first, but becoming gentler as he located a nipple through the fabric of my bra, and began flicking at it with his thumb. I shifted position a little, partly to allow him more access, but also to part my legs a little. I brought a knee up very slowly and gently, until I felt it make contact in between his legs, and then rocked myself languidly back and forth, feeling his warmth building through his trousers, and his excitement rise with the motion.

I kissed him hard. 'Let's go through.' The wall in the hallway has never struck me as the most romantic place in the world, not when I'd spent a fortune carpeting the rest of the apartment.

Barry nodded, and we tumbled into the living room,

his hands already fumbling at the last few buttons of my blouse. I reciprocated, stripping off his jacket until it dangled from one wrist, and then pulling at his shirt. He had already moved on to my skirt – I reached behind and released my bra strap; then, while he continued fumbling, I deftly unbuttoned my skirt and let it fall to the ground.

He'd already removed his trousers, and my eyes fell to his cock, straining against his jockeys, pulling the waistband away from his body. I reached out and jerked his underwear away; it snapped against the top of his legs, and my hands slid down to cup his balls.

He groaned as my palm skimmed across his scrotum, and my fingernails scraped the tightening sac, then he reached out to stroke my cunt through my knickers. Now it was my turn to groan, as his fingers sank through the soaking fabric. Hurriedly, I pulled them down, stepped out of them and crushed myself into his arms, relishing the hairs on his chest as they prickled my breast, and the force of his cock pushing hard against my stomach.

He felt so strong. A lot of guys can get so hard that you wonder sometimes why they don't rip their own trousers apart. But there's not so many whose cocks can actually pull at your hand, and make it move. I squeezed a hand between us, cupped the tip of his prick between thumb and forefinger, and rubbed him. The stickiness drove me crazy.

I stumbled backwards, tumbling on to the sofa, my

legs wrapping around him as I fell. I expected him to slide straight inside me; instead, he fell to his knees and, parting my legs, drew his tongue slowly up one thigh.

I squeaked and, with a hushed chuckle, he repeated the motion on the other leg, tracing the tip to my groin before flicking away. Again and again, he licked to the very edge of my pussy, and all the while his fingers danced against my hips, or stroked across my belly, or buried themselves beneath my ass, to draw me closer to his face. His nose brushed my clit and, for a moment, I almost threw myself into him, to bury my cunt in his face and grind myself to the orgasm that I knew was hovering so unbearably close. But I held back. Outside the video store, I told him 'You're the boss,' and, right now, that's what I wanted him to think.

His fingers were parting my lips, stretching them wide as his mouth brushed my flesh. He was sucking me in, first one side and then the other. My hips were moving gently now, my clit screaming out for the contact it craved and, as his hands pressed against my ass and lifted me, I couldn't have stopped my hands from clasping around his head, even if I'd wanted to.

He was licking me hard now, his tongue dancing across me, zeroing in, encircling, clockwise first, and then anti-, tripping and flicking and whipping around. A finger drove up inside me and I gasped aloud as he started fucking me with it, without once losing the incredible rhythm of his tongue. It was maddening, I was so close, so very, very – and then I was there, and I swear I levitated, that my body left the sofa and wrapped itself around his head, as my legs crushed his ribs and I was flying on his face, with every nerve end singing a different note.

I fell back, hearing the springs of the old sofa growl in protest, and he leaned across and kissed me hard on the mouth, my cunt juices still sharp and luscious on his lips.

I was jelly. I could barely move my tongue as his twined around it, and I couldn't even feel my legs. But I forced myself to lean forward, as my hands clasped his ass and I pulled him to his feet. His cock twitched before my face, still hard, but with a bright sheen of moisture coating its thick head. I reached out and grasped it, pulling him towards me, but he stepped back. 'No. You don't have to.'

I looked up at him. I felt the words on my lips – 'but I want to' – and then forced them back down. I jerked him gently, and then lay back against the sofa, cupping my breasts in my hand. 'Please … here.'

He smiled and stepped forward, lowering himself until his prick bobbed between my spread tits. I clasped them together, trapping him between them, saw his knob end poking defiantly out from the two mounds of soft flesh. And the words came tumbling out before I could stop them. 'Fuck me, Barry. Fuck my tits.'

He began moving slowly, carefully. 'Harder,' I breathed. 'Faster.'

He increased his pace, one hand cradling his weight, the other gripping the base of his cock, holding it into place.

'Faster. I want you to come all over my tits.'

He was losing it now, his eyes closed tight, his cock driving through my cleavage. I bent my head further, stretched my tongue as far out as it would go, and felt it make contact with the tip of his prick, a fleeting lash and the unmistakable tang of taste that made my pussy water as fast as my mouth.

Again, I had to taste him again. I clamped my hands on his ass so he could not withdraw so quickly, and, if he came just a little bit closer, I could fold his helmet between my lips, and, a little bit closer still, and I could suck this man dry. But then he cried out and his prick jerked away, and his come … It spurted this time, splashing on my tits, into my cleavage, across my nipple, thick and white and lovely, every drop tingling and tart on the sensitive flesh – and, as he fell back, so I sprang forward and pushed my dripping tit towards his mouth.

'Suck me. Please, Barry, suck me.'

His mouth closed around my spunk-soaked nipple, drawing it into his mouth and swallowing hard. He sucked, and then he licked; and then, as I crouched ecstatically above him, his mouth swept across my chest, devouring all the cream he had spilled there, so that, when I bent to kiss him again, there was only the ghost of his flavor on his tongue, and only the shadow of stickiness adhering to his lips. So I turned my head and, without a word, I scooped his semi-soft cock into my mouth, so deep that I could not breathe, and so warm that I didn't want to.

I sucked him as hard as he had sucked me, and rolled his balls in my palm until his hand told me to stop. He raised my head – there was a plop as his softness flopped on to his stomach – and gazed at me in wonder. 'I thought you didn't …' he started to say, but I hushed him with a kiss.

'I thought I didn't, as well. But maybe I do, now.' I thought of adding something – 'Of course, there's only one way to find out, isn't there?' – something like that. But it would only wind up sounding crass. I decided to tell him the truth. Or something like it.

'It was when I saw you … felt you …' I hoped I wasn't laying it on too thick. 'My breasts … I've always been afraid, in case I didn't like it. But then you did it, and I wanted it as well.'

He smiled. 'I've never done anything like that before. Never even wanted to. But the way you spoke, the passion … no one's ever talked to me that way before. I would have done – would do – anything you asked me to. And I loved every drop of it.'

I cuddled up to him on the carpet. 'I know exactly what you mean,' I whispered, and my hand fell on to his lap. He was hardening already and, judging from the twitch I just felt, I think we'll be sharing that glorious feeling again – very, very, soon.

And, if he says anything else, I'll just tell him I'm a fast learner.